Sir Little Cat

Guardians of the Mythic Castle

Johann Knörtzer &
Rebekah Connatser

For all the cat guardians.
Past, present, and future.

Table of Contents

Chapter One:
Recruitment Day

A dozen and a half or so stood at attention within the Eastline County Training Facility, doing their best to look presentable and fierce. This was the day when the King and Queen of Mythic Castle were to arrive and choose two personal guards from amongst the ranks of young warriors.

The trainees were cats, of course. That was plain for all to see. But none of *them* could have been convinced such a minor detail mattered in the slightest.

Fiddle stood near one end of the line, and held himself rigid as the royals entered, giving off no sign of fear. Jak, on the other hand, was doing his best to cram the last bits of breakfast in his mouth with the few seconds he had left. He was nudged by Fiddle, his brother, who was concerned the unprofessional act would rub off on him if anyone noticed.

"Brush off those crumbs, dummy! They're coming!" hissed Fiddle.

"Oh, you worry too much, Little," said Jak, using the nickname for his brother, which referred to his smaller size. "I'm sure none of us'll get picked, anyway. This is all for show to make it look like those robed fancy-pantses give a hoot about anyone way out here beyond their towers and walls."

Fiddle's expression did anything but improve, and Jak wiped his lips mostly clean while the royals continued their long greetings with the trainers.

"It very well *could* happen," said Fiddle. "We've trained harder than anyone else here. Well... *I* have anyway.

But you can be pretty funny sometimes, I guess. Maybe they'll make you the court jester."

Jak let out a fake laugh. "I don't even care, honestly. I'm not getting my hopes up. Though, I have spent some time thinking about what sort of foods they serve in that royal kitchen...."

"Yeah, you would," replied Fiddle with a quick pat on Jak's belly.

Jak half-turned with annoyance. "Hey! Keep your paws to—"

"Shush!!" cried Fiddle in a hoarse whisper. "They're coming over!"

The row of young trainees straightened up once again as the king and queen made their way past each of them, starting on the side furthest from the brothers. The two kept their eyes fixed straight ahead, not daring to take a peek down the row. Such an act of foolishness would only give rise to disappointment, if not outright suspicion. But they listened carefully and tried to pick up on any keywords of use. It was well known to them that no more than two would be picked out of all the lands to serve on the Royal Guard.

"I like this one!" bellowed the king. "She's got a look of confidence in her eyes, and quite a dazzling fur pattern if it's not too forward."

That was one down. One more to go. Fiddle's hopes weren't gone yet, but he always imagined his brother would be right there with him when he went into whatever service he'd inevitably enter. If the king liked her for her coat though, *his* looked almost identical. Maybe that would give an advantage. The voices went quiet again and the procession down the line carried on.

Any and all belief that Jak would be picked was long erased in his mind. He simply wanted to get it over with and return to his duties. He just wasn't cut out for this level of responsibility. Besides, who wants to be trapped inside a stuffy old castle after all—

"Well hello there, young man," said the queen, who was now standing right in front of him.

"Wha-huh-yeah?" Jak blurted out in startled surprise. "Uhh, hi... also."

The queen covered her mouth to hide her laughter. This was not going well at all. He couldn't seem to so much as form a simple sentence.

"And what, may I ask, is your name, trainee?" the queen said.

"Uh-umm," he stammered. What was his name, darn it? "Uh, J-Jak. I mean Jak. Just Jak. With a K only though, no C."

"Ah, a strong designation if there ever was. Now, what are your qualifications?"

"I can, um, whack the heck out of stuff

with this here sword I have pretty good. How's that grab ya?" His nervousness ended up turning him to humor, which may have easily appeared quite rude instead. He cringed at his word choice and the response he was about to receive.

The queen suddenly burst into laughter—so much so that she eventually had to pull out a folded cloth with which to wipe tears from her eyes. The king was chuckling as well. Jak gave a short, embarrassed laugh of his own and forced an awkward smile.

"You are hired!" the queen nearly shouted. "You have brought much amusement to me. Something I have been looking for in a recruit for some time." The king added nothing and was still chuckling.

Jak strained to keep his jaw from dropping, but his eyes went wide.

Fiddle kept his composure, but he

certainly shared similar feelings of surprise. Of all the things he'd considered could take place on that day, this was not one of them.

Jak nearly went into a panic. His thoughts went ahead, into that stuffy castle, and the possibility of never seeing his brother again.

"If you like *me*, you'd love this guy here," he quickly stated, nodding to his left. "This is Little, my brother. You'll find no one more dedicated to service and guardsmanship than he." The king stepped around his wife to have a look at Fiddle, then Jak added, "And we have always worked very well together, despite our differences."

"He does have that sleek black-and-silver coat I so much admire," said the king before going into a few moments of deep thought.

He turned to the queen, and the two

put their backs to the brothers and did more than a bit of whispering. Eventually, they turned once more with radiant and smiling faces.

"What kind of folk would we be to split up a pair of brothers so close?" asked the king rhetorically. "Jak, Little... the two of you have got the job. Grab your things and meet us out front at the carriages. I must go make amends with a young lady down the row. I'll put in a good word for her, I suppose."

Jak and Fiddle went to their bunks to fetch their belongings. As soon as they turned the corner, they began shoving each other and making hushed exclamations.

"This is unbelievable!" said Jak.

"I know!" replied Fiddle. "I was beginning to think this was our last day together. I just wish... that you hadn't told them my name was Little!! I could've strangled you! I was going to correct him, but it looked like he really enjoyed saying it."

"Eh, I'll let them know later," said Jak.

The brothers were packed and ready within minutes. They took one last walk through the facility they'd spent so long in, giving out farewells in the form of fist-bumps and head nods. They turned and bowed low at the door, then made their way out to the fancy wagon, which sat waiting to whisk them away to their new lives as Royal Guards.

Chapter Two:
The Road to Mythland

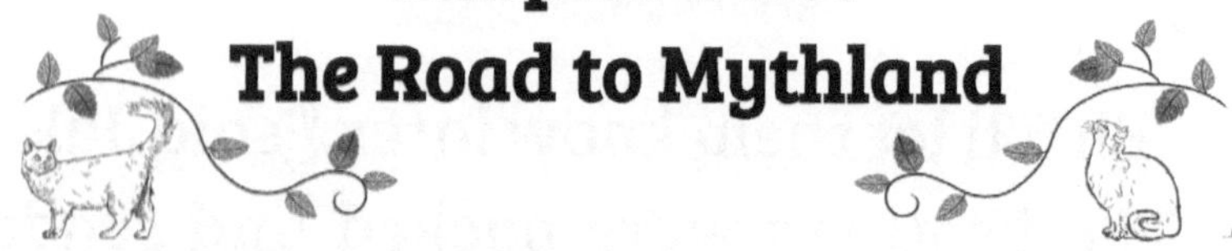

The village of Eastline had long faded from view of the twin carriages moving westward under the bright afternoon sun. The king and queen rode in the first, and their newly hired guards trailed just behind, bouncing along somewhat uncomfortably in motions they were not used to experiencing.

"I hope it's not much further," said Jak. "I don't know how much more of this shaking I can handle."

"Yeah," replied Fiddle, "it's not my favorite feeling. I've got to use a restroom soon. I forgot to go before we left, and this bouncing isn't helping at all." He leaned out the window and yelled up to the driver, "Hello, sir? Would you happen to know how much longer this ride will be?"

The man wiped his fingers across his nose, then shook his hand violently a few times before answering.

"I would say... just after sunset at least," said the man. "There may be a quick stop if you require the use of a pot. The king wants to swing by his grandmother's house to pick up some brownies and a couple of old coats. Not sure you needed to know all that, but now you do."

"Alright, thanks," replied Fiddle. He then turned to his brother. "You hear all that?"

"I got most of it. Did you ask how long *that* will be?"

"Ugh. No, I didn't. I don't want to annoy the guy."

"Would you ask, though? I'm really not feeling well. If it's too far, I might have to have him pull over so I can breathe a moment."

Fiddle rolled his eyes and grumbled. He was glad his brother was with him, but he'd been worried about when he would start making them look unprofessional and incompetent.

"I'll ask in a few minutes if we haven't arrived by then," he said. "I'm sure you'll be okay until—"

'BLEEEEHHHHH!!!'

Jak emitted an explosion of vomit, and not in any direction away from Fiddle. He tried putting his paw over his mouth, but was around thirty-five seconds too late for it.

"Are you kidding me?!" growled Fiddle.

"Sorry, Little, I"—he stopped to let out a small 'hhmp!' sound from a second wave that attempted to make an escape—"didn't think was going to happen that quick. I told you I was feeling sick!"

Fiddle was too irritated to even respond. Instead, he searched around for something to wipe himself off with. Unfortunately, he found nothing, and moments after he'd given up the search, the carriage came to a stop.

"We have arrived at the house of Lady Grammastola," yelled the driver. "Please remain seated until further instruction is given by the king and queen."

About two minutes later, the driver opened the carriage door on Fiddle's side. The queen was approaching.

"Oh, no!" he whispered. "She's going to see all... this! I'll be sent right back—I just know it. All thanks to you and your reckless puking!" He slapped Jak across the back of the head with a 'POP!'.

Fiddle tried to hide the mess, but the queen noticed it right away.

"Oh my," she gasped. "Did someone have an accident?"

"Well actually, Your Highness, it was—"

"Nothing to be embarrassed about, young man. It happens to the best of us. Come on inside Grandma Gramma's house and we'll see that you get cleaned up."

Fiddle nodded and climbed out to follow, as did Jak.

When the house entrance was reached, a quick explanation was given to the Lady, and she kindly pointed out the washroom to the brothers. They passed through with bowed heads nodding and offered a somewhat mumbled 'thank-you' each.

Jak received another earful of complaints in the washroom, and he continued to apologize for his careless aim. Eventually, Fiddle cooled off enough to drop it for a while, and the two made their way back to the main hall, where they were greeted with fabulous aromas. It was tempting to look into the source of such a magnificent smell, but they figured they should return to the carriage and wait.

"Hold up there, boys!" the king called out as the two were about to exit through the front door. "Come on in here and have a bite. We insist."

"There's plenty of pan-seared salmon to go around," said Lady Grammastola. "I made extra when I heard new recruits were coming by. Come in and sit down."

Fiddle and Jak looked at each other, then headed into the dining area to take a seat. There, they remained mostly silent, but ate their fill and listened to stories of older times, when the king was a young boy who refused to eat peas, rarely changed his pants, and could have never dreamed of becoming royalty one day.

When departing time neared, the brothers went out several minutes ahead of the king and queen, carrying multiple items the lady had given them. Such as a few tiny, empty green glass bottles topped with corks; four towels; some thick sweaters; long, striped socks; a stack of parchment; a bucket; and some kind of wooden puzzle cube. They were most thankful to their gracious host, especially since neither of them had ever been given anything they didn't exactly *need* before.

A little while later, the king and queen were back in their carriage as well, and the drivers called out that they were moving ahead once again.

The visit to Gramma's house had been longer than expected, and night began to fall well before entering the borders of Mythland. Fiddle was fast asleep with his head back and mouth wide open, and Jak was dumping his third bucketful of guessable contents out the window.

"I think it's finally easing up!" said Jak, not realizing his brother was out cold. "Little?"

Jak leaned toward Fiddle in the darkness of the carriage interior, but was less concerned with his snoozing sibling than what he saw out the window beyond. The lanterns on the outside of the vehicle briefly revealed a shape moving rapidly through tree limbs alongside the path. Whatever it was, it seemed to be covered in fur, much like himself, but far larger.

"Little!" Jak loudly whispered while pushing at his brother's shoulder.

"Huh? What? What do you want, puke-breath? I'm trying to sleep."

"There's something out there!"

"Hooey! You're seeing th—"

Fiddle was cut off as a huge furry arm

reached in from outside, seized him by the chest, and yanked him through the window. Jak was horrified and in shock, but quickly came to his senses as he drew his sword and pushed the door open to dive out and roll to a stop in the blackness of the woods behind the receding light of the still-moving carriages.

Chapter Three:
Denner Grey's Prowlers

Jak struggled to find where Fiddle had gone. His vision was pretty good in the dark, being a cat and all, but the cloudy night under a thick canopy of trees was doing him no favors.

Once he was fairly certain there was nobody on the narrow dirt path, he stilled himself to listen. A light crunch was picked up by his twitching left ear—the sound of a fallen branch being stepped upon no doubt.

"There," he whispered as he silently unsheathed his sword.

He crept up to a row of bushes past the path's edge and slid himself underneath them. He lay quietly and peered into a small clearing where he could make out a few moving shapes and muffled sounds.

"I won't ask you again, cat," said a voice with the tone of a canoe being dragged across loose gravel. "How many more guards are there?"

"Just me in the back carriage," said Fiddle, sounding uncomfortable and out of breath. "I think there were at least fifty or sixty guards in the other one—okay, maybe thirty. There's several more carriages still coming up behind though, so I'd probably get out of here if I were you."

A small torch lit up then—a dim, orange glow that sent shadows swirling around the surrounding trees. Jak could see Fiddle tied to one of them, and before him, holding the torch, was a massive and filthy wolf. Despite the creature being well on the smaller side of his kind, he still looked huge compared to Jak's tiny and helpless brother. He had to get him out of there.

"I don't believe any of that for a moment," said the wolf. "But we're not so stupid and desperate as to attack the king and queen directly. I wonder, however, what those two royal trespassing cheekloaves would *pay* to get their adorable little guardboy back? If they ever even notice you're missing, of course."

"I say we take him to the boss," said another wolf, who was emerging from around the far trees. "I not gonna get involved with something on this level without his say."

"Always kissing up to that tantrum-throwing gas bag, aren't you, Howlard? Denner's worthless hide smacking us around and keeping us just scared enough to stay in line. I think this could be my chance to prove to the Prowlers that I'm by far the superior leader."

"Wow. Why don't you just let that little cat know everything about us? Huh, Bayo?"

"It's Darkfang now, and you'd be wise to remember it. Especially when Denner gets what's coming to him."

Howlard chuckled at the name. "Yeah, we'll see, Mr. Fang. Until that day of entertainment comes, what do you plan to do with this cat exactly? You want ransom money, right? Who's going to send a message?"

"Getting a bit sore in my front left leg," interrupted Fiddle. "Would one of you fine gentlemen care to loosen it up a tad?"

Darkfang snapped his attention to Fiddle and quickly moved his way. "Keep your lips closed, cat, before you narrow down my dinner decisions for tonight." He planted a fist in Fiddle's soft belly, knocking the wind out and causing him to cough. Then, the wolf turned to his companion once more. "How about Mawlynn?" he asked Howlard.

"What? She's a kid! Arctis would have your pelt if you so much as brought up the idea of his baby sister running errands for you and your treasonous plans."

Darkfang took a threatening step toward Howlard. "Arctis is your good best pal, isn't he? And Mawlynn has just enough of a fair and innocent look to easily gain access to Mythland without being attacked on sight. You'll convince her brother in whatever way necessary, or there'll be trouble." He patted Howlard on the shoulder three times, letting his claws sink in a bit on the last one.

"Why don't we just ambush a remote farm or a passing wagon and force one of them to go?" asked Howlard with a wince.

Darkfang's eyes grew colder. "Because we can't trust what they'd do. They could track us back here or give the wrong information. Even if it were a good idea, I've already given an order, and I won't back down from—AHHHH!!!"

Darkfang howled in pain from Jak's sword stabbing into the top of his foot. Before either of the wolves could react, Jak had pulled the weapon free and cut the ropes that held Fiddle to the tree.

"There's another one!" cried Darkfang. "They're trying to escape! Seize them!"

"There could be more waiting in the shadows, Dark. We should let Denner know whether you like it or not. I don't wanna be taken out by a cat army tonight."

"Denner can suck dog biscuits! He's pathetic and weak, and his time is over! I am the new Alpha of the Prowlers!"

Just then, as Jak was helping Fiddle hobble down the path away from the crazy wolves, he heard the thunderous crash of splintering branches. He stopped to glance back through the bushes and saw that an enormous wolf stood towering over Darkfang.

"Gotta keep moving!" whispered Fiddle. "They'll catch us if we don't get far away from here!"

"One second," replied Jak. "I want to see this. We may have to deal with them again in the future," he leaned in and squinted to watch the drama unfold.

Two more wolves, one pure white, and the other a reddish brown, were moving in on either side of the enormous wolf.

"Pathetic and weak... was that right, Bayo?" roared the largest beast that was almost certainly the one spoken of prior. "Bayo, the dreaded 'Darkfang', challenging Denner Grey, Nightmare of Mudthorn Forest?"

Yeah, definitely him.

"What a battle it will be! Come now, I'll

let you take the first swipe. Arctis and Snarleen won't even interfere. Howlard won't either, if he still follows my orders and hasn't been swayed by your *mighty* influence.... Come on, tough guy! Let's go!"

Darkfang stared at the ground with teeth gritted and shook his head... just before Denner grabbed him by the throat and hurled him into the tree Fiddle had been tied to.

The wolf let out a yelp and stayed down, knowing he had no chance.

"Two... cats..." Darkfang wheezed out. "They were guarding... the king and queen's carriage. I captured one, but... another cut him free. They ran off just as you got here."

"Fool!" screamed Denner. "Are you trying to bring an entire army down upon us? Get your sad carcass up and help find them. They can't have gotten too far yet. We'll deal with this swiftly before they can fetch help."

Denner pulled a giant battle axe from his back and charged toward the woodland path with at least a dozen more wolves joining in behind him.

"Alright, I've seen enough!" exclaimed Jak. "Time to get the heck outta here!" He grabbed on to Fiddle's arm and the two ran.

Chapter Four:
Escape From Mudthorn

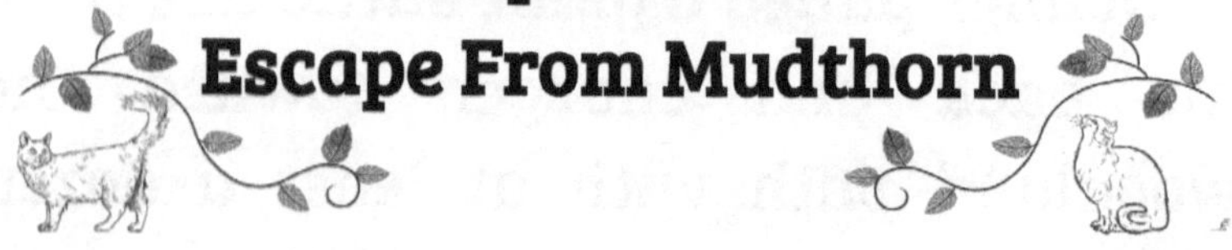

Jak and Fiddle bolted through the dark forest as fast as their legs would take them. They'd grown weary long ago, but they had to keep moving. Denner and his pack of wolves were still following them, only seconds behind.

"Have... to... stop... and... breathe..." panted Jak.

"I know it burns, just put it out of your mind and keep moving!" said Fiddle.

Not one more minute went by after those words were spoken, when Jak slowed to a halt and collapsed.

"Come on, get up!" cried Fiddle in a panic, hearing the thuds of wolf paws pounding the earth louder than ever.

He leaned down and shook Jak, then

tried to drag him, but it was no use—his brother was out cold. Unmatched in stealth, endurance was never one of Jak's better qualities. So, he rolled him over into a nearby pile of tall weeds, then lay down in them as well, hoping the wolves would pass by. But he knew better. The wolves would easily find them by scent.

He began muttering to himself. "Think, think! I've been training my whole life for this. Does it really matter how big my opponent is? I'm an expert swordsman, and I will defend us to the end."

Fiddle reached for his weapon, but found nothing there. Then he remembered loosening his sword belt in the carriage—it must've still been inside it. All was not lost, however.

"I'm sure you won't mind if I borrow this," he said to Jak, who was breathing heavily in his sleep.

Fiddle took Jak's sword and gripped the handle tightly. The wolves were right on top of them now, and they would hear the breathing as soon as they stopped walking.

"The prints stop here," growled Denner. "They must have turned off. Spread out and find them, NOW!"

A loud sniffing sound was nearing Fiddle's face. This was it—his first and probably last fight. His arm trembled as he prepared to take a hard swing of the blade to Denner's nose. But, just before he could, he noticed it was not the leader of the pack. Instead, it was the one who'd pulled him from the carriage and tied him up.

"Hold up," whispered Fiddle, causing pause and mild surprise to Darkfang. "I heard you talking about that jerk, Denner, and I don't know why any of you listen to him. You're twice the leader he could ever be—five times even!"

"It's been established that you're a liar, and a terrible one at that," replied Darkfang. "Why should I spare you another word?"

"Because I'd like to live, and I'm willing to do anything for you to help me make that happen. I can bring you money from the castle, or better yet, I can do the exact thing you were afraid of!"

The wolf snarled and showed his teeth, growing far beyond impatient. But Fiddle kept talking.

"Get anyone who's loyal to follow you out of the area, and I'll have the army come and sweep the woods! No more Denner, and you won't even have to fight him to become the new Alpha. They can be sent first thing in the morning."

The wolf thought about it for a moment.

"How do I know you won't send them

tonight and wipe us all out? You know too much."

"Fine, don't believe me. Fight me now then—and if you manage to beat a professionally trained swordsman who's been working his whole young life for a moment like this, then you can have me for dinner and go back to being Denner's dumb little stooge. We both know you can't overthrow him on your own."

Darkfang's face turned angrier by the second. Fiddle expected him to call out or try to grab him, but he calmed himself, speaking slowly and softly.

"What do you want me to do?"

"Tell them all to follow you the other way. Say we ran that direction."

"And you'll have Denner taken care of tomorrow?"

"Sure thing."

"Alright. Deal. But I'll still shred you apart if I see you back in these woods once I'm running things. Remember that."

Fiddle nodded, and he noticed Jak was beginning to stir.

Darkfang sprang up and darted down the path, and within two minutes, Fiddle heard him yelling, "I found them! This way!" as his voice trailed off in the distance.

"Jak!" Fiddle hissed in his brother's face. "Get up now! This is our only chance!"

Jak blinked a few times, then nodded and jumped to his feet. "Okay! Let's go!"

The two ran once more, but Fiddle, upon turning onto the path, smashed face-first right into something wiry and hard. It was the meaty and fur-covered leg of Denner Grey.

"Guess I'll have to teach that double-crossing traitor a serious lesson later on," said the massive wolf. "But first, I'll deal with you two. No more games. It's time to end it."

The wolf jumped forward with his axe swinging down hard. Fiddle sidestepped and turned it away with Jak's sword, causing the wolf's weapon to sink into the dirt. He quickly yanked it free, then swiped low. Fiddle shoved Jak into the bushes while skipping in the air over the axe at the same time.

"Run, Jak!" cried Fiddle. "Get to the castle! I'll hold this brute where he stands!"

A rustling was heard that soon faded away. Jak was gone.

"I'll catch him once I've chopped you to bits, don't you worry," said Denner.

The two clashed again. Fiddle, with fast and precise movements; Denner, with slow-but-deadly, powerful strikes. There wasn't much Fiddle could do to bring down such a large foe. He needed a well-placed thrust to do any real damage. The axe blows were easy enough to dodge for one so agile as he, but great caution still had to be taken.

After several minutes, Fiddle's pace wore down. He'd gotten some pokes and cuts in, but nothing serious. All it took was for a simple, unexpected kick from the wolf to his gut, and Fiddle found himself windmilling backwards, struggling not to trip, then lay himself sprawled out on his back.

Denner came in quick at this vulnerable moment, taking another forceful swing that Fiddle desperately tried to block as he continued to stumble, but his grip had weakened, and the sword fell to the dirt.

Fiddle let gravity take him, and he did a backwards roll, coming to a stop in a crouched position... a few yards away from Jak's sword. It was all over now.

Should he run? Or face these overwhelming odds with dignity and courage.

Denner smiled as he lifted his axe one last time. Fiddle stood to his feet and stared him down, ready for whatever came next. The wolf laughed, then screamed in agony.

"AAHHHHHHH!!! Get it off!!!"

The wolf spun in circles, waving his axe around until it flew from his grasp, then he reached his huge paws back to his tail, where Jak's teeth were firmly latched on.

It took five hard, painful yanks, but Denner eventually pulled the cat from his tail. He lifted Jak up, squeezing him by the throat in a furious rage.

"Bite my tail while I'm not looking, huh?! HUH!?! Well, have some of this then! You wretched little pest!"

Jak choked and flailed about, his

vision growing dark. But Fiddle was already coming to his brother's aid. With sword in paw, he ran up the front of the giant beastly canine and swung with everything he had, tearing a long slash into Denner's face and across his right eye. The wolf immediately let go of Jak to clap his paws over the wound, then fell down, rolling and kicking on the ground.

Fiddle and Jak continued their sprint once more, and kept going until they were out of the forest. They slowed to a brisk walk when they felt they'd put enough distance behind them. The open fields surrounding them, though dark, provided a wide view of any would-be attackers from there on.

Soon, they passed fences and farmhouses until, finally, they saw the flickering lights upon the castle walls.

Chapter Five:
A New Home

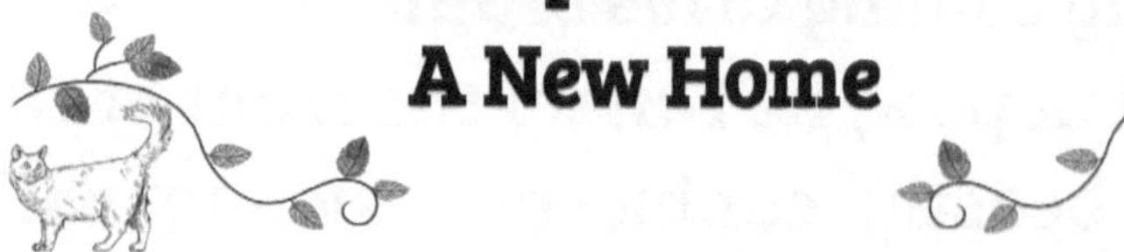

The encounter with the wolves had not taken as long as the brothers thought. When they arrived at the castle gate, it was sitting wide open with the carriages parked just inside, still being unloaded. The king and queen were talking with the drivers, and did not look concerned or confused. Perhaps they hadn't checked the rear carriage yet, but it looked as if they might at any moment.

The cats crept up to the back of the vehicle, and Fiddle went to peek around the side to see if they were clear to climb back in. He pulled his head back when he saw the king coming his way, but it was too late—he'd been spotted.

"Out already, I see," said the king, the

queen now trailing just behind him. "I hope the rest of the ride wasn't too hard on you boys."

"No, uh, we were just stretching our legs back here a moment while you finished up with the drivers," said Fiddle, suddenly concerned whether or not he should say anything about what truly happened.

The odds were stacked heavily against them, sure, but it wouldn't be good to hear of the new guards being defeated and having to run away before their first official day began.

Besides, he'd thought it through and the problem was likely to sort itself out. Those dirty mutts would never come near this place. They said it themselves.

"What time will dinner be?" asked Jak, bringing more chuckles from the royal couple.

"It is a tad late," said the queen, "but we

can have something whipped up for you, especially after that dreadfully long and bumpy ride. Come, I'll put an order in for some roast chicken, and while you wait, we can show you around your new home." The king winked and gave a thumbs-up in agreement.

The brothers were led through enormous front doors and into a long main hall that branched out to other corridors on either side at intervals of about twenty feet or so. The queen went ahead, evidently to address the cooks, while the king pointed out artifacts and paintings which hung on the walls as they followed him further in. He continuously gave details about decorative pieces that were mildly interesting at times, though he alone seemed completely fascinated with all of it.

"And here we have a painting of the

record-setting fish I almost caught in my youth," he explained. "The line was broken as I was pulling him from the murky depths, but I got a good look at the fellow before he plunged back from whence he came. Over here, you'll see a framed replica of the broken line and a scale model of the rod I used."

"You really like fishing, huh?" said Jak.

"Can't *stand* the rubbish nonsense if I'm being honest," answered the king. "But I did almost set a record. Now, if you'll look just down the hall a little further, you might notice a painting of the queen and I with the famous minstrel, Fredribald Lutestrum. We met him when he played at the Etiquettorium in Ronaldsburg several years ago. He even signed my third best ceremonial shield hanging right there, if you can believe it. Terrible musician really."

"You're going to bore them to tears

with your old stories, dear," said the queen as she came back to join them.

"Who is this?" asked Fiddle, pointing to a portrait of a gray cat with hard eyes.

The queen walked slowly over to Fiddle and stood beside him, a look of seriousness washing over her.

"A previous guardian," said the queen. "His name is Pierre. He'd been with me since I was still Princess of Cartareth. He stayed in my services for a time after I was married and came to live here, but became bored with the closed-in walls and nothing much to do.

He desired adventure, and to face down threats out in the wild, rather than wait indefinitely for something to happen here. Last year, he left on good terms with our blessing. We heard he had joined a mercenary outpost in the far south who regularly clash with groups of raiders down there, but that's all I really know. Perhaps he'll come back to visit us one day and you can meet him."

Everyone stood in thoughtful silence for a while until Jak decided he could not contain the question on his mind.

"When you say there was nothing much to do," Jak began, "and he might never see anything 'happen' here... what does that mean, exactly?"

The queen waved her hand around, gesturing to the stone building they were currently within. "This place has never been attacked. No one has ever tried in the many decades it has stood, and we've no reason to believe they ever will. We're not sure why. We have no guards aside from you two, and no army has ever served us. If we'd had a problem before you came, we would have simply called the local authorities to sort it out. The guarding position is mostly ceremonial, I'm afraid. I'd hoped you would find the lack of danger appealing. We still would like someone to keep watch at night and while we're away, but I cannot promise you'll ever need to take any action."

"Fine with me!" Jak said with sincerity.

"I'm sure it'll be okay," added Fiddle. "We couldn't have asked for a better place to be sent, and we truly thank you for this grand opportunity."

The king and queen looked at each other and smiled, then said 'you're welcome' in two very different ways—enough so that they were both forced to stop and try it again, one at a time.

Right after, the king began sniffing at the air with widening eyes. "I'd say that chicken is nearly ready for you!" he exclaimed. "Let's go get you seated in the dining hall."

The group proceeded to where the hallway ended, opening up into an enormous room. It was well lit, decorated with hanging plants and further weaponry and shields. More paintings of various cats were seen, as well as a few life-sized statues. Four massive pillars held the high ceiling in place thirty or so feet above, and between them, on either side of the main aisle which cut through the room on a velvety red runner, were many tables and chairs. A fireplace crackled and roared on each side of the room, and at the far end were two thrones set high atop a pedestal.

The brothers found a cozy enough spot, and soon, a server brought plates and cutlery, followed soon after by a silver platter, upon which rode the crispy, juicy, shining golden remains of a plump flightless bird.

"It's all yours," said the queen. "Have as much as you like. When you're finished, we'll show you to your quarters."

The dinner was pure excellence,

perhaps even somehow better than the fish they'd had for lunch. If this was how the royal folk ate day to day, then this job just might be okay.

When they'd finished, the king showed them to a room down one of the side halls. It was far larger than the bedroom they'd shared with ten to fifteen other cats at times. They'd even each have their own dressers, nightstands, chairs, and plenty of open space to themselves here. It was almost too much to comprehend.

"There are other rooms available in case either of you ever need a break from the other," laughed the king. "Goodness knows I've used them."

The queen jabbed him in the ribs, then spoke. "Get all the rest you like. We may go over some scheduling, look into future events, or possibly just tour the castle a bit more tomorrow. No need to put a rush on things. And please, do make yourselves at home. We consider you two a part of our family now. See you in the morning!"

She walked out, and the king grabbed the doorknob to pull it closed for the night. "Goodnight, Jak. Goodnight, Little." And the door was shut.

"You'll let them know, huh?" said Fiddle.

"It was a busy day in case you forgot," replied Jak. "There's still plenty of time to set it right. Now avert your eyes while I change into my jammies."

Chapter Six:
Terror in the Night

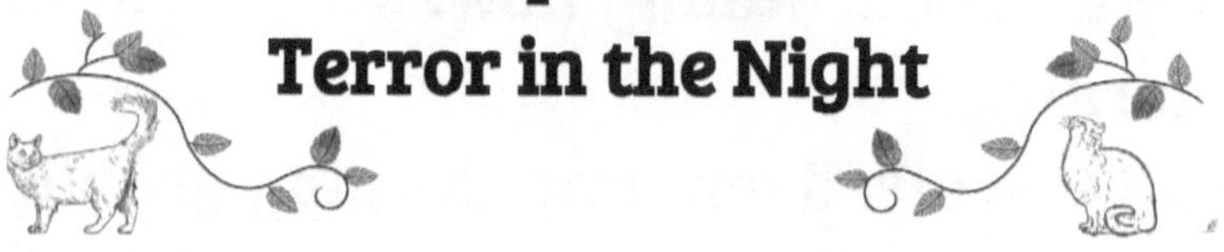

The next day came... and went. Not much happened, aside from touring the gardens, the ballroom, the library, the ramparts, and the seldom-used armory. Over the following weeks, the brothers did plenty of standing at attention, greeting harmless and well-known guests, and doing lots of eating.

After three months of a routine like this, they began noticing a touch of flub swaying before them as they walked. So, they got back to training to keep themselves fit and sharp. Just in case a forced entry or an assassination attempt occurred for the first time in the castle's history. It couldn't be ruled out, no matter how safe the king and queen believed they were.

Another three months had gone by when, one night, Jak and Fiddle were sound asleep in their room. Until two weeks earlier, one of them would have likely been keeping a night watch, but the practice was seemingly quite pointless. However, Jak's mind was changed rather quickly when he was jolted awake by a loud crash from a not-too-distant part of the castle.

"Fiddle?" Jak softly called out.

His brother did not stir.

"Fiddle!"

Still nothing. Jak slowly slid himself out of bed and tiptoed across the cold floor to Fiddle's place of slumber. Thankfully for him, Fiddle was there, breathing quietly in a deep sleep. No other noises were heard, and Jak felt foolish and wondered if he should even bother him.

'CRASH!'

"Fiddle!!" He seized his brother by the arm and shook him violently. "Wake the heck up!"

Fiddle tossed, turned, sat up, rubbed his eyes, and blinked hard at Jak.

"Whhaaaaaat?" he asked with great annoyance.

"I heard sounds. Banging sounds—coming from the kitchen, I think. We should go check it out, probably. Unless you don't need me, that is."

Fiddle yawned, then nodded with eyes still half closed. "All right. Let's grab our gear first. And yes, you're coming."

With swords at the ready, they crept out of their room, taking care not to let the door creak. They made for the end of the hall, stopping where it met the large dining area so they could look around.

"See anything?" asked Jak.

Fiddle shook his head and waved for

him to keep following.

Once they entered the kitchen, the two stayed low and silent as they scanned for signs of intruders. Evidence presented itself right away, in the form of three pots strewn across the floor near the oven.

"Maybe the cooks had them stacked, and they just fell," said Jak, hoping it was true.

"Could be," replied Fiddle. "But look over there."

He motioned to the other side of the kitchen, where a pile of cutlery lay out in a similar fashion. His mouth opened to verbalize the observation, but he was cut short when another noise was heard—crackling and tearing. This one was not nearly as loud, but it left little doubt that someone was indeed very near. It came from beyond the far corner of the room, through an open doorway leading into the pantry. A place that overflowed with profound darkness.

Low-burning lamps and streams of moonlight entering various windows had dimly lit each area the cats moved through up to this point, but no such beneficial illumination could be detected inside that room.

Fiddle searched around until he found a candle on a counter, then held it to the flame of the closest lamp. The wick burst to life, and the two proceeded once more toward the unknown sound.

The candle threw an orange glow past dancing shadows of shelving and boxes as the pantry was entered. Right away, they both spotted something out of place. A ripped bag on a middle-height shelf that contained some sort of powder for baking. A steady stream of white was pouring to the floor from the bag's open corner, causing a light cloud to rise and further impede visibility. Fiddle stepped around the growing mound of powder, and Jak did the same.

The room was fairly large for a place to simply store food—at least in their minds. But there was still a reasonable limit to places they could search.

More disturbances were found; a pile of napkins on the floor and a spilled sack of potatoes. They searched down each wall, then over and under each shelf and cabinet, expecting some crazed murderer to spring from every spot they checked. The two were baffled. There were no windows or vents, and the doorway to the kitchen was the only way out.

"I have no idea," said Fiddle, with a shrug and a sigh.

"Well," said Jak, "there is another thing it could be."

He looked as if he was growing sick

with the thoughts coming to mind.

"No," replied Fiddle. "We're not even going to discuss anything like that. I'm sure there's some explanation. A draft, or small earthquake could have caused... some of this. Let's just go back to bed and check in the morning. We'll talk to the cooks and see if they've experienced anything like this before."

"We should probably check the other halls and rooms first. I won't be able to sleep until I'm sure no one is lurking around in here."

"Right. That's reasonable. Let's g—"

They both saw something move. A wisp of translucent white rose from floor to ceiling near the entrance, where it came to rest, hovering and rippling like a tattered flag.

Fiddle was frozen, but Jak was backing away. In doing so, he rolled his foot over a misplaced potato, which sent him stumbling, then crashing into a shelf. As soon as he did, the mysterious apparition darted through the doorway and made a sharp turn around the corner.

A moment later, Fiddle came to his senses and shouted, "After it!" then ran out of the pantry.

Jak was reluctant, but did not want to be left alone. So, he gripped his sword tight and followed Fiddle out and through the kitchen.

"Fiddle!" he called out as he ran. "That was a ghost if I've ever seen anything. What would we even do with it?"

"I don't know. But we have to make sure nothing can be done before giving up."

They caught sight of the fluttering tail of the thing as it quickly moved out into the main dining room, prompting them to sprint harder before it could get away.

It crossed to the hallways on the other side, going beyond their own room to the corridor's end, then seemed to pass straight through a solid door.

"In here!" said Fiddle, making his way to the room and finding the door to be locked. "Let me grab the keys from my nightstand. Keep an eye out and hold the candle till I get back."

Fiddle dashed away, and Jak did his best to keep himself from violently trembling as he focused on the shiny black knob, imagining it suddenly turning.

'CRASH!' 'BANG!'

Whatever was inside was not happy. Jak shuddered to think of the horrors that would greet them once the door was opened. His mind conjured up images of long teeth in massive jaws, blood-red eyes, a dozen arms with spindly fingers waiting to grab him by the tail.... He felt a touch on his shoulder and let out a yelp. It was Fiddle.

"Step aside," he said. "I found it."

The key was inserted and turned with a few noisy clicks, then Fiddle drew his sword again and kicked the door wide open. A freezing chill burst forth from the place, as if death itself had taken up residence within.

No searching would be necessary this time. As soon as the brothers stepped through the threshold, the pale specter rose from the floor in the center of the room and stretched itself out to look down upon them. It wavered and rippled in the air like nothing they'd ever witnessed. Nothing... that was... except for the one exactly like it near the far wall, being illuminated by moonlight entering through a broken window.

"Broken... window?" Jak asked no one in particular.

"Curtains, both of them," said Fiddle. "But how could this one move in such a way?"

They noticed that there were a few chairs and small tables stacked tightly together just under the first floating cloth in the center. Fiddle made his way around them to inspect the underneath. Something was moving in there.

"Candle!" Fiddle called out.

Jak moved in closer and held the flame-topped stick near the tangled mess of chair legs, lighting up the floor between. There before them, in plain view, was a gray mouse furiously chewing at a twisted corner of the curtain that was wrapped securely around its back foot. The creature was nearly free, so Fiddle reached in with haste to grab it.

His paw was met with a painful sting, causing him to recoil. The mouse had half a sharpened toothpick outstretched, ready for another strike. Fiddle angrily reached in again and flicked the weapon away. Then, he seized the mouse and pulled it out, using the cloth to wrap its whole body to prevent further movement.

"Unhand me, beast!" screamed the mouse before spitting in Fiddle's eye.

Fiddle gritted his teeth and squeezed the rodent until his eyes bulged.

"You're trespassing in the royal halls, rat," hissed Fiddle. "I'd love to end you right here and toss your carcass out the window. But I'm afraid you'll have to be locked up for the night instead. You'll face the king and queen in the morning and answer for your crimes."

The mouse spit in Fiddle's eyes twice more each and protested, but Fiddle smacked him over the head with the handle of his sword, knocking him out cold. He was taken back to the guard's quarters and locked inside a small wooden box with some holes in the top.

"Now we can finally get some sleep," said Jak, throwing himself into bed. "No ghosts after all."

"Yeah, but at least it *felt* like we got to experience a little action for once. It had my blood pumping there for a bit, honestly. Can't wait to see what the king thinks of this thieving little pest. That should make for some entertainment."

Fiddle stared at the box for a while, then put out the light and rolled onto his own bed.

***

'CLACK!'

The wooden box landed on the stone floor at the foot of the king and queen's thrones.

"Caught a trespasser rummaging in the kitchen last night," said Fiddle. "Figured we'd let you decide his fate."

"Good work, Little," said the king. "Let's have a look at this intruder."

Fiddle carefully unlocked and opened the box, finding the mouse still inside. The tiny creature had partially shredded apart the wrappings, but was still mostly incapacitated. He looked up at Fiddle with hate in his beady eyes. The mouse was lifted by his restraints, and held aloft for the royal couple to examine.

The king leaned in for a closer look, but the queen slid as far back into her throne as possible, a look of uneasiness spreading across her face. Jak moved to stand beside her for comfort.

After a few minutes passed, the king asked the mouse a question.

"What is your name? And what business do you have in our home? Speak quickly."

"Wanna know my name, eh, crowny boy?" replied the mouse with a tone of exceeding rudeness. "Well, I'll tell you. It's Spippy! Spippy Pipperpepple!" With every 'P' sound, the mouse heavily sprayed spittle on the king's face. "And my business here is... to do this!"

'POO! POO!'

He fired off two more large spit wads, which crashed into each of the king's eyeballs with a 'PSH! PSH!'.

Fiddle was sure this mouse was about to get flattened out good. The king reached over and grabbed... his handkerchief, then dabbed at his face.

"Just take him out to the gates and send him on his way," said the king. "He is very impolite, but we need no prisoners nor spilled innards in this castle. Off with him."

Fiddle was disappointed, but he did as

the king commanded. He carried the mouse that may or may not have been named Spippy well outside of the castle grounds, then untied him.

Still gripping him tightly, Fiddle brought the rodent up to his face and spoke in a harsh tone.

"I don't ever want to see you back here. Got it? You've been extremely fortunate today. Remember that. Because you won't leave here a second time."

Spippy worked up some phlegm, readying it for launch. But Fiddle slapped his head sideways, then wound up his arm and threw the mouse as far as he could. He watched the creature disappear into the distant morning sky, then drop below a row of bushes.

Fiddle wiped his paws off, then went back inside.

"Well done," said the queen. "You both finally got a chance to prove your worth as royal guards, and gone beyond expectation."

"It is time then," said the king with a wink at the queen.

The king stood and walked slowly over to a display case by the nearest wall. He opened it and lifted a glistening sword from its velvet-lined interior. As he walked back to his throne, he called out in a loud and attention-seizing voice.

"Guards, step forth!" he cried, motioning to the area directly in front of his stopping point.

Fiddle and Jak hurried to the spot.

"Kneel!" shouted the king.

They did so, and the king lifted the sword above them as if to strike them down. But nothing of the sort took place. Rather, he lowered the blade, tapping it lightly on each of Jak's shoulders.

"I knight thee, Sir Jak the Chivalrous!" He took a step to the side. "I knight thee,

Sir Little the Valiant! Stand and be witnessed as official knights of Mythland. May you honor us with many years in our service."

The king clapped a firm hand on Fiddle's shoulder in congratulations while the queen embraced Jak and told him, "Good job, Buddy."

The knights were given papers, pins, and medals to signify their new status, then treated to a dinner of flame-broiled ribeye steaks.

Chapter Seven:
Howls of Wrath

All was quiet again for months until one evening after the king and queen had gone to bed.

Jak was already asleep, but Fiddle decided to grab himself a snack and go on a short patrol. He made a poor attempt at whistling as he carried a lantern down dark halls, through empty rooms, and across high ramparts.

Eventually, Fiddle began yawning and figured he'd better get to bed before he ended up passing out in some cold random place. So, he started back toward his room.

A moment later, a noise was heard that caused his ears to twitch. He tensed up and listened closely. It was a scratching sound, quiet and constant. Fiddle silently followed the noise, lowering the flame in his lamp and staying close to the floor. He considered waking Jak first, but he was sure he could handle this himself. Jak would probably just be terrified and make a racket.

The scratching continued, and led Fiddle to an upstairs room near the center of the castle, just below the royal bedroom. It was more like a utility closet with its small size, and rarely visited for any reason.

Fiddle stood outside the closed door, listening to the awful sound. It was if someone were trying to saw a piece of metal in half. Hesitantly, he turned his lantern back up and threw open the door. There was a stack of boxes and other unused items piled against the back of the closet, and atop of it sat a white mouse, furiously rubbing a small stone back and forth across the wall.

"HEY!" shouted Fiddle.

Before he could get another word out, the mouse threw the rock at him and bolted. Fiddle pursued, enraged and determined to destroy the intruder.

Tables were overturned and decorations knocked around as the mouse stayed just one step ahead, weaving and sprinting through various halls, then down and back up stairways.

At last, the mouse came to a dead end, and threw itself into a tiny crack in a stone wall. It wiggled violently, trying to force its back end to follow.

Fiddle yelled like a crazed person and drew his sword, then struck at the mouse's rear over and over. Sparks flashed and chunks of rock flew from the wall, but the mouse had slipped through. He punched the stone angrily and regretted it right away.

He thought of the window in the nearby room and moved to it, trying to get a look outside. The full moon lit the courtyard and the outer walls, and he could just barely make out a tiny white dot moving toward the main gate. If only he could see exactly where the mouse was heading.... But he could.

There was a small seeing-scope on a shelf in the study room he was currently within. He grabbed it and put his eye to the glass.

The mouse squeezed through another spot in the outer wall and moved on toward the distant woods. It was getting difficult to see, but it looked like the rodent stopped at the treeline as if speaking with someone.

Then, he saw him.... The Nightmare of Mudthorn Forest: Denner Grey. He'd been conversing with the mouse from the shadows, and now emerged, followed by many, if not all, of his Prowlers. They were making their way straight to the castle.

Fiddle's eyes went wide. "I've got to wake Jak!"

He tore down the darkened corridors at top speed, sliding to a stop at his bedroom door, which was quickly thrown open.

"Jak! Jak!!" he called out.

His brother's snoring ceased, but he did not answer. Instead, he rolled over and pulled a pillow over his head. Fiddle darted to the bedside and ripped the pillow away, then shook and yelled at Jak with terror in his voice.

"GET UP, IDIOT! WE'RE UNDER ATTACK!"

Jak bolted upright.

"Wha? By who?"

"It's Denner. He and his Prowlers are

making their way to the castle. We've gotta do something."

"But... if it's the whole pack we'll be hopelessly outnumbered."

"Then we'll have to make them think we aren't. Come on. I've got a stupid idea."

The brothers ran around to many rooms, grabbing different yet specific objects and setting them in certain places—mostly near windows. As often as possible, they'd take quick looks outside to see how near to the castle the wolves were.

"They're going slowly," said Fiddle. "They think they're being stealthy. Probably going to go for one of the front windows by the direction of movement. Shoot... looks like there's fifteen or twenty of them. Just a few more things to set in place. Let's hurry!"

Dozens of thin ropes were attached to some items they'd placed, then run out to the halls and joined together. Finally, the opposite ends were tied to a larger rope that looped through a mechanism for hoisting curtains, then cranked tightly.

Fiddle finished setting up a line of mirrors in the main hall, then doused all but the smallest of lanterns, sending the castle's interior down to an unsettling darkness.

Then, he and his brother drew swords and sunk into the shadows to listen and wait.

***

"This is the one," said Arctis as he approached a damaged window a dozen yards to the left of the main door of Mythic Castle.

"Good," replied Denner. "Snarleen, come up here and get this window open—and I don't want to hear a sound."

The female wolf nodded and eased herself up to the poorly patched glass panes, then pulled out some tools from a pouch hanging from her belt. In moments, small circular holes were made in the glass and the latches were flipped. She took out a bottle and applied its liquid contents to a brush, which she used to thoroughly coat the inner edges of the frame.

After waiting about a minute for the concoction to do its work, she slid the window up noiselessly.

"After you," she said with a wave.

"Howlard can go first," said Denner, "then Arctis, then me. The rest can follow however they like."

The wolves quietly filed through the opening in their designated order, taking note of the layout and trying not to knock anything over.

"What was that?" asked Howlard, head

spinning all around.

"You're hearing things," replied Arctis. "All jumpy from the stories you've been listening to about this place. It's all made-up garbage. Now quit blabbering and check what's through that door."

Howlard crept over and opened it carefully, peering out into the near lightless hall beyond with a rusty hatchet raised overhead. He saw nothing and motioned for the others to follow. But halfway down the hallway, he stopped abruptly and held up a paw.

"I swear to you I hear whispering," he said.

Denner pushed Arctis aside and leaned in close to Howlard, growling in his ear, "The two cats are their only protection and they are rarely up all night. That's what we were told. Are you afraid one of them is going to pop out of the shadows and poke you with those little toothpicks they carry? If you can't handle this, then get behind me."

Howlard put his head down and moved to the back, letting Denner take the lead.

Almost all the wolves were filed in line behind Denner now, and he was nearing the main hall. Just a few more steps and he'd be—

'SNAP!'

Denner suddenly fell to his face and began rapidly sliding backwards, knocking the Prowlers to the floor in a flailing heap. He went all the way to the far end before slamming the wall. Disoriented, he tried to stand, but heard a quick 'SNIP!', then another 'SNAP!'. He tumbled onto his back and took off down the hall again in the other direction, bowling the line of wolves over once more before most had even got to their feet.

This time, however, he continued through the main hall and disappeared into the darkness of another hallway across the great room, snarling and clawing the air the whole way.

"I told you!" whispered Howlard. "We need to get out of here!"

Arctis had no time to answer. A sudden glow of a hundred pairs of yellow eyes lit up from all around the main hall, then a startling shout pierced through the still silence.

"GUARDS!! ATTACK!! LEAVE NONE ALIVE!!"

Many of the wolves ran back the way they'd come in immediately, including Howlard. But Arctis hesitated a moment when he saw torches light up ahead of him. An alarming sight was revealed in that moment: cats, many dozens of them. All had swords raised, ready for action. That's all he needed to see.

He bolted back to the first room, pushing past a few other Prowlers before diving out the window and sprinting for the gates. Soon, all the wolves were out of the castle and headed toward the woods. All—that is—except for one.

Denner finished chewing through the rope around his ankle and raised himself up. He was slightly afraid, but very enraged. The newly lit torches showed the floor before him. Now he watched for any more traps.

Stepping out into the main hall, his rage grew even more. His companions had deserted him. All because of what he stood in the midst of. Several carved statues of armed cats lined each side of the path between the halls, and mirrors gave the illusion of their great number. Yellow marbles were tied to their faces as well. Evidently made of a very light-sensitive glass that caused them to glow under the faintest flame. He proceeded to the room's center and scanned the area for movement.

***

"Ready?" asked Fiddle. "I'll take the left leg. Go!"

He darted forth from the darkness, sword trailing behind and Jak running beside him. The two reached Denner and swung hard at his meaty calves, slicing in deep.

The wolf roared with anguish, then swiped his great axe at them. But they were too quick and moving in different directions.

Jak circled back around and stabbed him in his furry side, but Denner seized him by the throat and held him high, raising his axe to meet his tender belly.

Fiddle came in fast and jumped,

cutting into the arm that held his brother, opening the deathly grip and causing him to drop to the floor.

"It's time," said Fiddle. "Go!"

Jak disappeared into the shadows once more, and Fiddle took off between statues and mirrors, heading towards the castle's giant front doors.

Denner pursued Fiddle, leaping past obstacles and closing in quickly down the entry hall.

Fiddle swerved to one side and swiped a shield from the wall with a jump, then kept on running until he reached the door. It was already open just a crack, and Fiddle slipped through, out into the front yard.

Denner flung the doors open with a 'BANG!', then spotted Fiddle running down the stone path that led to the gates. The wolf picked up the pace and caught up in no time. Fiddle tripped and fell face-first to the ground, then scrambled to his feet again with sword and shield ready.

"I will split your fragile little body clean in two," growled Denner with a hint of a smile.

It was then that Fiddle noticed the dark bandage over the wolf's right eye. The eye he had slashed during their last meeting.

"You shouldn't have come here, Denner," said Fiddle in the most commanding voice he could muster. "I'm an idiot for saying this... but I'll give you one more chance to leave and never return."

Denner chuckled. "What an adorable offer. But I'm afraid I must decline. I know you've got no defenses. I'll kill you and the other guard"—he took a quick glance behind—"then bring the others back. This castle will belong to us by sunrise. Good riddance, fuzzy."

Denner's legs were having a bit of trouble from the wounds. He wobbled and stumbled forward, axe raised and ready to strike.

It came down in a flash. Fiddle smashed it away with the oversized shield he carried, then slashed at Denner with his sword before the axe could be raised again. Nothing was hit.

The wolf began swinging from the sides. Left, then right. Each time, Fiddle jumped back a little more, keeping an eye on the ground just beneath him.

"This accursed thing is too slow," said Denner. "Let's try this one."

He threw down the huge axe and pulled a long and jagged knife from his side, then lunged at Fiddle faster than expected.

Fiddle took several lengthy hops back as Denner closed in and slashed wildly. After five or so, he spied what he was looking for: two sticks laid in an X shape. He took one more jump back and threw his sword at the approaching wolf. The blade sank deep into Denner's shoulder, making him come to a halt and pull at the lodged-in weapon.

The sword was yanked free and tossed away. Fiddle had nothing but his shield now.

"You're finished, boy," growled Denner with fury in his good eye.

The wolf took one step forward, crunching the crossed sticks under his foot.

"NOW!!!" screamed Fiddle, just before dropping to the ground behind his large shield.

Denner's eye widened for a moment at the thought of what it could mean.

The command echoed through the front door, down the entryway, and up the stairs to the second floor, where Jak stood. He was trembling with anticipation, and as soon as his brother's voice reached his ears, he swung his sword, cutting the rope in front of him clean through. The frayed ends shot down the hall and spread out to several rooms, then up to windows where the other ends were fixed to the strings of loaded bows. The tension was released, and the arrows fired, all pointed directly at the crossed sticks.

It all happened within two seconds. Fiddle felt the thud of an arrow hit his shield, along with the sound of many others finding a mark elsewhere. He peered over the top of the shield to see Denner with his mouth hanging wide open. The knife clattered to the ground and the wolf's eye rolled back. Then he collapsed on his face, his back filled with protruding arrows.

Fiddle stood and retrieved his sword

right away, then went over to the wolf's body and gave it a few pokes. He leaned down, listening for breathing, then hesitantly feeling for a heartbeat. Nothing.

Jak came running up just then.

"Is it over?" he asked.

"Yeah, he's done. And I doubt his friends will ever be back here to find out after what we pulled off."

"What do we do now?"

"Get a shovel while I figure out how to move this to somewhere discrete. I don't want the king and queen knowing about any of this. We stopped the threat, and they've got no reason to live in fear."

It took a couple of hours, but the wolf and his belongings were moved to a secluded location just outside the wall, and it was all buried and covered over.

"Now to get all those statues, mirrors, and other junk put back before the sun comes up," said Fiddle.

"Don't forget about the other traps we didn't use," replied Jak.

Fiddle sighed.

It took a couple more hours, but everything was set back in its proper place and cleaned up. Jak was sent to bed twenty minutes earlier since he'd nearly broken a few things while falling asleep standing up. Now, Fiddle was wiping one last cat statue clean and longing for sleep himself.

"Well, you're up early!" came a sudden voice.

It was the king.

"Yeah, just tidying up," laughed Fiddle.

"Oh, don't worry about that, Little. The cleaning lady can get it."

"Okay," said Fiddle, and dropped what was in his paws back onto the floor with a clatter.

"Anyway, I've got some other things I'd

like to go through with you since you're up. Then, perhaps you can accompany me to the market. I need to purchase some parts to fix that front window, maybe get fitted for a new pair of sleeping pants, and grab a big jar of pickles for the queen. She's had a strange appetite lately."

Fiddle sighed again, then nodded.

Chapter Eight:
Four Years Later

"We're going to be late!" yelled Fiddle. "Hurry the heck up!"

"Yeah, yeah, just one more quarter-minute and I'll be ready," replied Jak.

Jak had been trying to dry out his long fur for what seemed like hours after taking a similarly long bath. At any moment, the king and queen would announce their departure to the nearby town of Dusket, a place which held an annual festival and parade to celebrate something that probably happened a long time ago.

It was not an event the royal couple usually attended, but today they had been convinced to go by their young daughter. She'd been all smiles and could barely sleep the past few nights in anticipation, telling her baby brother about what they could expect to see there, but getting only babbling and spit bubbles as a reply.

"Jak! Little! It's time to leave!" the queen called from outside the brothers' door.

"We should have been waiting for them at the door!" said Fiddle. "Let's go."

Fiddle made his way out, and Jak got a few more brushes in before running after him, still pulling his gear on. The two filed in beside the royal family as they made their way outside. Then, all six of them entered the royal carriage. The driver snapped the reins, and the vehicle rolled down towards the gate behind the clopping of horse hooves.

Fiddle stared out the window, to the place where he knew Denner Grey's body lie under the earth. He and his brother had faced several intruders and challenges of various kinds over the last four years, but none so terrifying as that night. The royal family still knew nothing of what took place then, and at times, Fiddle wondered if keeping it a secret had been a good idea.

For now, he needed to put all that out of his mind and focus on the day ahead. This day would be marked as the first time the king and queen had brought both of their very young children so far from the castle, and extra caution would be necessary. He began scanning their surroundings and running scenarios and plans through his head in preparation for anything.

He was just imagining a great beast tearing the top of the carriage off when he felt a poke in his side. He snapped out of his deep thoughts and looked to the source of the interruption.

It was the princess. She had her arms crossed and was looking away as if she'd no idea what Fiddle was searching for.

"Yes, my lady?" said Fiddle with extra softness in his tone.

The princess let out a giggle, turned around, and yanked Fiddle close to her.

"Aww, Little Cat," she said.

Fiddle looked across the carriage interior to see Jak in a similar situation with the young prince, while the queen smiled down at them. As much as he and his brother cared for the king and queen, these children were something truly special, and they would gladly protect them until their last breath.

Fiddle allowed himself to relax and lean into her, but he still kept his eyes turned toward the window.

***

The group had been at the festival for a couple of hours, playing games and winning cheesy prizes; riding various exotic animals, including a zebra that got into a heated argument with Fiddle; and eating strange, new, delicious treats, such as bananas on a stick covered in crunchy, sugary rock-like candy. All that was left to do was find a good spot to watch the parade.

They found one and had been standing together for a few moments when the princess started fussing.

"I gotta go potty!" she said.

The queen sighed. "Alright, let's go find a restroom."

"I'll go," Jak said to Fiddle.

The queen asked around until someone pointed her to the restrooms. It was a large barn type building with two doors on the front. The queen guided her daughter through the door on the left labeled 'Ladies', and Jak stood just outside to keep watch.

A few minutes went by, and Jak saw a huge black bird land on the roof of the building. It was some sort of scavenger by the looks of it, like a buzzard or vulture. Or were those the same thing? He stared at the weird and scruffy creature for a while until... he heard a scream from within the barn. It was the princess. He ran to the door and pushed it slightly open.

"Everything alright in there?" he asked.

"Yes," said the queen. "We're coming out. There was a huge rat in here, is all. It ran away."

As the queen exited the restroom holding the princess's hand, Jak noticed there were more birds on the roof, just like the first one he'd seen. More than a dozen of them stared down at them, eyes hard and fiery, like they were up to no good.

The next thing Jak knew, several birds were swooping down with talons opened wide, heading straight for the princess.

He drew his sword and leaped at the flying menaces, swinging this way and that, sending feathers flying.

"FIDDLE!!" Jak cried while thrusting his blade into a bird's gut.

Fiddle and the king heard Jak's call and rushed in his direction. But Fiddle told the king to get the young prince back to the carriage at once. He hesitated, but decided it was best to trust his guard and turn around.

Fiddle reached the area and immediately saw the danger. He went straight into action and took three birds down with a quick series of jumps and swings.

"Get them back to the carriage!" Fiddle

yelled to Jak.

Jak nodded, grabbed the queen's hand, and started running.

Most of the birds continued swooping down at Fiddle, but one exceptionally large individual broke from the swarm to follow the escaping group.

"Jak! Watch out!" cried Fiddle.

Jak felt powerful claws grip the back of his neck and lift him from the ground. His paw slipped from the queen's hand. He looked up to see that the princess was held by the other talon, and was screaming wildly. He knew he had to do something quick.

The queen was running under the bird as fast as she could, and thankfully, they were not yet terribly high. Jak twisted himself painfully and swung his sword at the bird's other leg. It was cut clean through, and the child dropped toward the ground.

"Catch her!" yelled Jak.

The princess hit the top of a cloth tent, bounced and flipped over a few times, then rolled off the edge into her mother's arms. She looked to be unharmed.

The flying devil shrieked and thrashed about, making it quite difficult for Jak to get a good hit on the leg that held him, especially from the awkward position.

As he took another swing, the bird kicked and rolled over, causing Jak to lose hold of his weapon. The sword plummeted down, blade piercing the earth within feet of an old lady eating a bundle of fried celery.

Jak squirmed, fought, waved his limbs about, but there was no getting out of the bird's iron grasp. All he could do was hang helplessly while the town of Dusket faded into the distance.

A good deal of miserable time went by while passing over various landscapes, and eventually, the flying creature swooped low, likely in approach to its destination.

Jak was pinched into a rear-facing position, and could not tell what he was headed towards, no matter how he strained to turn his head. He began imagining all sorts of terrible things and tried giving one more effort. He flailed his limbs and scratched at the bird's remaining leg. Then he twisted and howled in anger, trying to swing his weight and throw off its balance. But nothing seemed to work.

At last, things grew dark as Jak was carried through a large opening in a stone structure and finally released to a cold, hard floor. He rubbed at the back of his sore neck, feeling the burn of his wounds.

The bird bounced and flapped, attempting to adjust to its new lack of a foot, as it hobbled across the room to sit and stare at him. Its gaze slowly turned to the shadowy depths of the room's far corner, where multiple sets of eyes were alight with a menacing fire.

One particular set stood apart from the rest, which looked somewhat human to Jak. And soon, a sound issued forth from where those eyes lay.

"Take him to the dungeon," commanded a raspy, crackling voice.

Immediately, a fox and a raccoon stepped out from the dark, seizing Jak by the arms with alarming strength. The animals each had a near lifeless expression on their faces, and their fur was greasy and matted.

As he was dragged over to a door, Jak's eyes could barely make out the other shapes that stared at him. They ranged from half his size to more than five times bigger, by his guess. But right in the center, a withered old woman stood hunched over a crooked staff, half smiling, half frowning. Long clumps of silvery-white hair were draped across her pale face and down her shredded, decaying cloak, almost touching the floor.

"Welcome to my home," she mumbled through a mouth of ruined, yellow teeth. "We've been looking forward to a visit from Mythland for a long time."

Jak was given no time to reply. The fox and raccoon shoved him through the door and down a hall, where they came to a spiraling stair and descended for what felt to him like ages. And when the bottom was reached, one of his captors lit a small torch to cut through the thick blackness.

He tried to struggle once more, but found his strength to be all but spent. So, he hung limply and awaited whatever came next.

Without a word, the other animals shoved him through the door of a small cage, and it was quickly slammed shut behind him. Then one pulled a chain nearby that hoisted the cage up to the ceiling.

"What do you want with me?!" screamed Jak. But the two simply turned and walked away, sending the room into total darkness.

Chapter Nine:
The Two P's

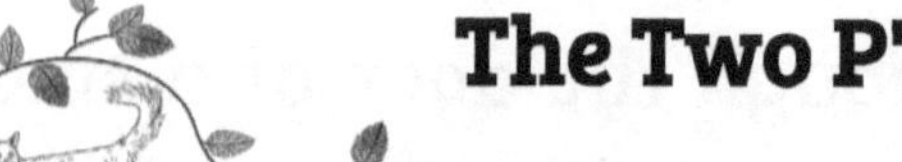

Fiddle watched as the king and queen took their children inside. They were back to whatever safety the Mythic Castle could provide for them. They were down by one guardian, but would soon have none to protect their home.

Once the children were taken to their rooms, the royal couple spoke with Fiddle briefly at the front door, knowing how urgent the task at hand was.

"I can join you in the search," said the king.

But Fiddle shook his head. "No. You need to be here with your family. We don't know who's responsible for this and they could take advantage of this situation. I will find my brother—

whatever it takes."

"You two are part of this family," said the queen, her voice quavering. "You have been since you arrived. Make sure you both return safely. Not for the services you provide, but because we love you and want you here with us."

The king nodded in agreement, then stooped to rest a hand on Fiddle's shoulder.

"I know you can handle this, Little," he said," but do be careful out there. We'll be in touch with the local authorities and see if they can assist in any way."

"We'll come back safe," said Fiddle. "The ones who took him would be right to worry. See you soon."

He turned and dashed off, through the gate, across the edge of town, and into open fields washed over with the reddened light of the sinking sun.

***

"Hey..." said a hushed voice from the blackness of the dungeon, not too far from Jak.

He hesitated to answer at first, but finally gave in after hearing it twice more.

"Yeah?" he replied.

"Who are you?"

"Not sure I should tell you that."

"Well, I'm a prisoner too. I used to be that horrible witch's servant."

"Used to be? Guessing you two had a disagreement."

"I did everything she asked, but she was mostly decent then. She went crazy a few years back—maybe even longer ago—and started locking up everyone who'd helped her here, sometimes torturing and experimenting on us. As you saw, some of the other animals don't act natural... at least the ones allowed to roam about the tower freely."

"Why'd she go crazy?"

"No one is sure. Might've had something to do with a feud she got into with royals over in Mythland. But I can't imagine what could've set her off that badly."

Jak gulped at the mention of his home, then answered, "I was a guard there at the castle, and the witch certainly knows it. Seems she brought me here for that reason alone. Though, I don't know why. My name is Jak, and—" he lowered his voice—"my brother is coming to get me out of here, I'm sure of it. We can get you out as well."

"Really? I haven't seen the light of the sun in so long. I'm frightened to even think of it. I could go blind. Though, I must admit I have been fortunate compared to others here. I've been left mostly alone, aside from a few experimental spells and elixirs that wore off with time. She's been going through those mice like you wouldn't believe."

"Mice? The castle was broken into multiple times by mice just before a large attack by wolves! Were they the same ones? If so, what were they trying to do?"

An eerie chuckle came from the darkness below them, then a voice, the one belonging to the witch.

"It took years of trial to get those blasted rodents even temporarily immune to the defense spell on the castle. I suppose I outdid myself when creating it. A mistake that will never be repeated. Every one of the mice I sent in was killed by its effects, including the one who finally erased the carved rune that broke the spell. And I'm guessing the king and queen tossed out all the poisoned food once they found out a mouse had been in their pantry.

Even my elaborate plan of getting the wolves inside failed. But now that I have one of their beloved guards, I think I may be able to complete my revenge on those uppity, cake-chomping, better-thans. Just you wait until your brother gets here—I've got a surprise for him! Now quit talking to the other prisoners before I turn you into a handbag. And I don't even need magic to accomplish that."

"What did the king and queen ever do to you?!" yelled Jak.

There was no answer.

"Hey! Lady!" he cried, voice echoing off the walls. But the witch had seemingly departed.

Jak stayed silent for a long while, well into what he assumed to be the middle of the night, before trying to speak again. He kept his vocal noises to a bare minimum this time.

"You there?" he whispered.

"Yeah," replied the fellow prisoner from before.

"If you don't mind my asking, who and... *what...* are you?"

There was silence for more than a few moments, enough that Jak nearly asked again, but a reply was given.

"I am a cat. My name is Popeil. Some just call me Pope. Though crude insults are all I've been addressed by these days...."

"Well, Pope, I wonder if these cages will touch if we both get them swinging hard enough? Feels kind of rusty. Maybe we can break them."

"I don't know. The sounds would be risky. I can't imagine what she'd do if she found out. And you never know when she's lurking down there. She could be there right now."

"If she's got a trap set for my brother,

he needs to be warned. We've got to try something. Listen, we can stay quiet for a bit to play it safe, then I'll give three taps. Start swinging away and towards me as hard as you can and I'll do the same."

Popeil let out a sigh. "Alright."

Jak counted to one hundred several times in his head, all while wondering if this pause before trying his plan would be better or worse for them. Then, he tapped one of the bars with his claws three times, and right away got to swinging his cage. He leaned forward and back, and could hear the creaking metal of the other cage in front of him.

After some time had passed, he thought the cages might be too far apart. But no sooner did the thought cross his mind than he felt a powerful jolt and heard a loud 'CRASH!'. They'd hit.

As his cage was shaking and wobbling to a stop, he felt around for damage. One bar was bent somewhat severely and cracked. He thought it could be close to snapping.

"A bar is broken," he called out quietly, "give it one more try and I might be able to slip through."

He tapped three times again and started the routine over. This time, after the initial crashing sound, another one followed it. It was a large chunk of metal colliding with the floor below. Jak felt the sides once more, but nothing had changed.

"Pope?" he whispered.

"I'm... out," said Popeil, his voice coming from beneath Jak. "I can't believe it. I... don't know what to do. It's too dark for me to see."

"Can you find the chain to lower me?"

Minutes went by before Popeil replied.

"I found it, but I don't have the strength to turn the crank. Even if I could, I've still got no way to get you out of there."

"Just go then," said Jak. "If you've got any memory of the layout in here, then try to sneak out and find my brother. His name is... Fiddle."

"Alright. I'll do my best. Just hang in there... err... sit tight.... Sorry, nothing sounds appropriate. Hopefully, we'll meet again."

"You bet," said Jak with a heavy sigh.

***

Fiddle had spoken with many a wild creature in the three days he'd been traveling, trying to find out anything he could about where his brother might be. A deer told him she'd seen some large, strange birds to the north a few days earlier, possibly on the day Jak was taken, so he continued on in that direction.

Another full day was coming to a close, and he was making his way through a fairly open forest when he noticed something move in the distant shadows of some thick bushes. He quickly got low and slid over to a tree to peer around it. Nothing was there.

"Maybe I'm seeing things," he mouthed to himself.

He hadn't slept but for a few short naps that couldn't have been more than an hour each since he'd left the castle. He wanted to keep going, but he'd be no good to anyone sleepwalking.

After a few yawns and watching the suspicious area a while longer, he slid down against the tree and let his eyelids slowly fall... until he heard a rustle nearby.

He bolted upright and looked around the tree again. Nothing. So, he stood and scanned the area. He'd never get any rest without being sure there were no murderers or bandits about.

All seemed clear, other than an odd shape in a tree about thirty feet away. He was trying to avoid looking directly at it, but he could've sworn it looked like a creature crouching up there.

It moved. Fiddle could now see a gleaming blade in its grasp. He clenched his jaw and attempted to keep calm, then put a paw on the handle of his sword.

The thing flew from the branches, landing right in front of him.

Fiddle wasted no time. He drew his sword and began slashing in a wild frenzy. Each strike was deflected by a weapon unlike anything he'd seen before: two opposing blades whose handles joined at the hilt, creating a single sword that could easily be spun with great speed.

He twirled and thrusted. Then rolled, dodged, flipped, hacked, and kicked, but could not land a hit. He pulled out his brother's sword and went full force with both blades.

Now he was gaining the upper hand. So much so that his opponent began yelling for him to stop. But Fiddle would offer no mercy to this treacherous beast. Nothing could stand in the way of saving his brother.

"WAIT, DARN IT!" yelled the stranger.

The two of them stepped away from each other, still holding their weapons at the ready.

"What?!" cried Fiddle, while finally getting a look at his attacker.

"Are you Fiddle?" asked what was now seen to be a scruffy gray cat.

"I *am*. Who wants to know?"

"I was looking for you. Someone told me your brother was locked up in the witch's dungeon. He said you needed help and to warn you of traps."

"If you wanted to help, then why the crap did you attack me?"

"I was just jumping down to ask if you were the one I was sent to find. You most definitely attacked me first. I simply kept myself from getting hit by your sloppy moves. If I wanted you dead, you would be."

"Sloppy?! I'm tired, alright? I've been walking for days with very little rest."

"Okay, okay. Don't get yourself all upset. I'm gonna help you get your brother out of that place. It's dangerous as all heck, but I know my way around some parts of it. I'm Pierre, by the way."

Fiddle's jaw dropped. "Pierre? I've heard of you."

"Yeah, you're the new guards for the king and queen of Mythland. Figured they might tell you about me. But if

you've got questions, they'll have to wait.
We need to get to the witch's tower, fast."
"Just lead the way."

Chapter Ten: Tower of Horrors

A rising full moon pierced the wispy clouds over Palemist Wood, casting a dim but unmissable glow on an ancient watchtower protruding up through the treetops.

"There it is," whispered Pierre. "Wraithwatch, it's called by some. Don't ask why, I don't know. But I've heard it was once a place where human soldiers were stationed to keep an eye out for invaders from the far northern mountains. It was abandoned for at least a century before the witch found it and took up residence. I thought I'd never get this close again."

"How do we get in safely?" asked Fiddle.

Pierre motioned for Fiddle to follow, then crept up to a boulder at the start of a slope that led up to the base of the tower. He sat a moment before pointing to a certain spot.

"If we can sneak up to that arch and scale it," he began, "making sure to stay out of view of the main entryway, we might be able to jump to that window ledge and hang on. There's another window further up, to the right. We could possibly reach if we're able to climb to the top of the first one without being seen. Looks like some jagged places beyond that may serve as footholds, but I can't be sure until we're up there, unfortunately."

"It's a plan, I guess. After you."

The cats silently and cautiously followed the steps laid out by Pierre, and soon they came to the messy, rough patch of bricks around the far-right side of the tower. They were about thirty-five feet up, clinging on with all their might to what little edges they could find there.

Every once in a while, the entire tower seemed to shudder with a boom coming from deep inside.

"What is that?" asked Fiddle.

"I have no idea," replied Pierre. "But I'm sure we'll find out soon. There's another window up there—a small one. A bar is missing out of it. Perhaps we can slip through if we can reach it. Give me a push."

Fiddle climbed up next to Pierre, then put his paw up for him to step on. The gray cat launched himself upward and grabbed the ledge, then leaned down to help Fiddle up. The two peered inside the dark room for some time until deciding to slip through the bars.

They were in what appeared to be nothing but a storage area, with cobweb-covered barrels and boxes stacked along the side walls. It was unoccupied and had a single door opposite of the window. A door which was, thankfully for them, unlocked. It opened to a dimly lit landing of sorts between ascending and descending stairs, all surfaces there made of damp, rough stone. Fiddle looked to Pierre for guidance.

"Like I said, I was told he was in the dungeon," said Pierre. "That's going to be all the way at the bottom. We'll keep following the stairs down, stay quiet, and slip into the shadows if we hear anything. Be ready to fight if we're spotted though, and don't hold back, no matter what comes at us. There are strange enchantments on some of the animals here. Let's just hope your brother isn't one of them yet."

The pair moved downward, Pierre on the right, and Fiddle taking it wide on the outside left. Within a minute, they'd crept down to another landing, this one with a door.

Before either of them could make a decision to investigate or pass it by, the knob turned. Pierre waved Fiddle over to his side, and the two huddled behind the door as it swung open. The hefty wooden slab noisily creaked while swinging, then came to a halt right at the cats' noses. Pierre held up a paw between their faces, letting Fiddle know to wait. Then, the door quickly jolted away, going all the way back around until it closed. They saw nothing there, but gave it a few minutes before proceeding once more.

"Careful," a growling voice echoed from further down.

The cats paused, watching intently. They heard nothing else.

After going down a little further, Fiddle pointed out a thin rope running across the path. It ran up the wall and attached to multiple blades tucked against the ceiling. It was put there just for them.

"Good eye," said Pierre. "I doubt it'll be the last one."

Fiddle nodded, and they kept moving.

Eventually, the stairs ceased, and the wall to their right ended, opening up into a wide space. They'd reached the ground floor.

"Your shift's over, we'll take it from here," came that same voice from before.

Some mumbling was heard, then the sounds of light footsteps approached the end of the wall where the cats were crouched in wait. Pierre rapidly waved for Fiddle to get back up the steps.

As they silently sprinted upward, Pierre slowed a moment to see what was coming. There were two figures, twice their size at least. They looked to be a goat and a coyote—each of them with various deformities, stitched wounds, and chunks of rusted metal protruding out across their bodies, some of which seemed almost to be holding the creatures together. Fiddle caught a glimpse of them too as he cautiously stepped over the trap rope. Pierre followed, and they stayed low and out of sight, both knowing what must be done.

Fiddle looked at Pierre and nodded, then Pierre reached out his blade and swiped it straight through the rope. The cats flattened themselves to the jagged steps as the large and wicked blades broke free from the ceiling. They felt the rush of air from them passing mere inches over their backs, and a moment later, heard the awful sound of their potential assailants being struck down.

"Go!" commanded Pierre, and the two bolted back down the steps.

They squeezed past the still slowly swaying blades and around the mangled wreckage of the two beasts at their feet.

"Keep moving," said Pierre. "Make for the next stairway down. It should be straight ahead if we keep following the outer wall."

"What was that?!" came the growly voice from the far side of the dark room the cats were running across.

Fiddle glanced over just in time to see a bobcat coming at them with a crooked spear. He thought about running harder, but a wild boar carrying a long saw slid in between them and the door to the dungeon. Both animals were just as grotesque as the ones from their previous encounter.

"No good," said Pierre. "We've got to fight them. I'll take pig-boy."

He sprinted at the boar, jumping to the left and running down the wall with double-bladed sword whirling. Then, he leaped through the air and brought the weapon down hard. The boar deflected it, but was too slow for the follow-up strike which struck his wielding-arm. This forced him to take it in his left hoof, and just barely knock away a further attack before it could skewer his rounded gut.

Fiddle himself was nearly run through as he watched the action, having already forgot the incoming danger. He twirled to one side as the spear thrusted past him, then raised his sword to retaliate.

"This is the end of you, kitty," snarled the bobcat. "Gonna wish you'd never set foot in this place!"

The spear connected with Fiddle's incoming blow, sending the sword sideways. It almost slipped from Fiddle's paw, but he grasped it tightly and moved in closer to gain advantage over the long weapon.

The bobcat was slashed across the right leg, and Fiddle was stabbed in his side. There was blood, but it didn't seem too bad from what he could tell during the commotion. It wasn't until the blade of the spear slipped past Fiddle's face and cut his cheek that he drew Jak's sword from his other side. He jumped away and waited, staring down the bobcat with all the fury he could muster.

He made a quick twitch to his left, and his enemy took the bait, beginning an upward thrust in that direction. Jak's sword was swiftly slapped against it, and Fiddle rushed forward while using the blade to keep the spear away. He gave the blade a downward push, then jumped atop the shaft of the spear, sliding down the length of it until he met the bobcat face-first, and rammed both swords into the wretch's undefended abdomen.

Fiddle rode the spear to the floor as the

bobcat loosed it, and with a short gasp, the beastly cat's eyes rolled back. He then toppled over, crashing into the stone floor with a soft, yet sickening 'thud'.

Fiddle stood over his defeated foe without a trace of satisfaction on his face. He felt nothing but disappointment and wondered if this creature could have still been freed of his curse, and returned to some kind of normal life. Did he have family, hoping he would come back to them one day?

This witch needed to pay for the evil things she had done to these animals. But his mind went to Pierre just then, and he turned to see if his companion needed help.

"About time you finished with that," said Pierre as he stood next to the fallen boar and wiped his blades clean. "Let's keep moving."

Fiddle nodded, but heard another

voice from upstairs.

"What happened here?!" it shouted. "Idiots must've forgotten and tripped the rope... I only told them ten times."

Pierre tried to open the door to the lower stairs. It was locked.

"Wait," said the voice above. "This rope has been cut! There's an intruder! He's here! Go! Go! All of you, spread out and find him!"

"Check the bodies for a key!" said Pierre.

Fiddle sprinted to bobcat and checked his belt. There was a whole set of keys hanging there. He cut the ring off and headed back to the door.

"I'll have to try them all," said Fiddle. "Just watch my back."

Pierre nodded.

The first key didn't come close to fitting, nor did the second. Still several more to go. Footsteps were clattering down the stairs behind him. It wasn't the third, the fourth, the fifth, or the sixth. Just one more to try. This last key slid in smoothly, but refused to turn. Fiddle looked over his shoulder in time to see over a dozen animals of various kinds coming around the wall at the base of the stairs. He jumped, planting his feet against the wall and put his weight into it, twisting the key with all his might.

'CLANK!'

The key turned.

Fiddle dropped, pulled the key out, and ripped the door open, pulling Pierre through with him just as he was raising his weapon for combat.

"Grab the handle!" cried Fiddle, and Pierre did so.

The door slammed shut and Fiddle jammed the key in and gave it a quick turn, locking it once more. The fiends on the other side shrieked and pounded, but

the cats wasted no time continuing their
descent.

Chapter Eleven:
A Search in Darkness

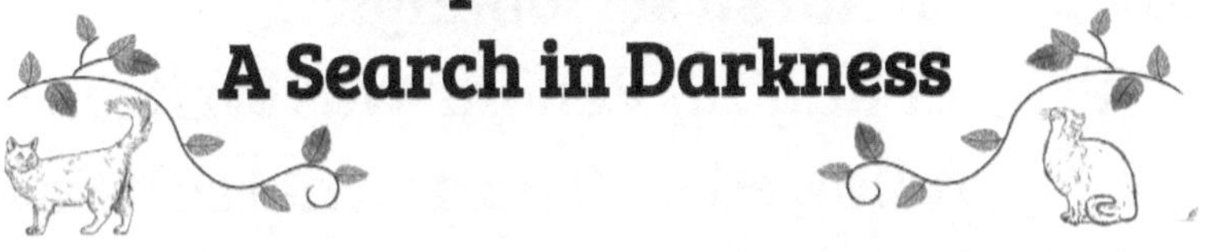

The stairway eventually ended in a fairly small room which was dimly lit by a low-burning oil lamp set upon a table on their right side. Carefully, the two searched. There had to be another door leading into the dungeon. Pierre felt his way down the left wall, and Fiddle moved toward the illuminated table.

There were things piled all over the table, but Fiddle couldn't quite see, so he hopped on a nearby chair, then right up onto the table itself. There were papers, books, herbs, rocks, and many jars filled with unspeakable things strewn about, and more still upon surrounding shelves. In the center, seemingly the object of most interest to what likely utilized this space, was a yellowed sheet of paper covered in harsh scribblings.

'Project Raging Venom' was written at the top, followed by lists and notes below. Fiddle skimmed over the random plants and disgusting artifacts listed there, not understanding what any of it could mean. So, he skipped to the bottom, not knowing why he hadn't walked away yet; he obviously was in no need of a gruesome recipe for who-knows-what. But on the last line were the words 'In case of bite' with an arrow pointing to the paper's edge, as if the answer lay on the next page.

"Might as well," he thought, but his action was cut short by a terrible sound from behind. It was Pierre, and he did not sound okay.

"Fiddle, get over here, now," he croaked in a hoarse whisper.

Fiddle jumped down and headed over

to join Pierre, who was crouched low to the floor next to a large box.

"Get down!"

Fiddle obeyed and asked, "What's going on?"

"Shhh! She's up there! This is a bed, and she's asleep in it!"

Fiddle's eyes widened. "What do we do?"

"See those crates in the corner?" asked Pierre, pointing to the area.

Fiddle nodded.

"I think there's a door behind them. Stay close, and stay quiet. Let's check it out together."

They crawled over to the dark corner and slipped around the crates. Pierre was right. Not only was there a door, but the key was already in the lock.

"I believe this is what we've been looking for," said Pierre as he turned the knob.

The door opened with a light squeak, and a snort came from the bed behind them, followed by a loud exhale and the clearing of a throat.

Pierre closed the door as quietly as he was able, making sure to take the key with him, lest they be locked inside. But as far as he could tell, there was no keyhole on the opposite side to keep her from following them. They'd just have to be quick and hope she did not wake up.

The next area was much larger, and very dark. A thick iron door was set into the lefthand wall, and Fiddle walked over to it to peer inside. About ten feet down a hall on the other side... was another thick iron door, and nothing could be seen beyond it.

Fiddle shook his head. "I hope he's not in there. We'd never get these open without—" He stopped and looked at Pierre. "Let me see that key."

Pierre handed it to him.

Fiddle lifted the key and moved it to the keyhole in the door. It was so much smaller that it could have probably fallen into the hole and been lost.

"Well, I tried," said Fiddle, handing the key back. "We'll have to check the rest of this place. If we don't find him elsewhere, then I guess we'll have to force the witch to give us the right key for this. And I'd rather not have to do that. I don't think we could win."

The cats moved into the deeper dark of the enormous dungeon, occasionally giving low whispers to call for Jak. There was a lot to search, and a thought came to Fiddle's mind as they walked.

"You said you've been in here before, right?"

"That's correct," replied Pierre, "but not down here. Only some of the upper rooms."

"May I ask why?"

Pierre sighed heavily. "I suppose I could tell you. It's not a pleasant story, though."

"I understand. I'd like to hear it, if you're willing."

"Years back, the witch used to frequent the town of Mythland. She was said to be a kindly person. I never figured out why, but she eventually had a falling out with the king and queen one day during a long visit with them. She had a suspicious look in her eye as she glared at me while I was escorting her off the castle grounds.

I knew not to trust her after that, but some months passed and we were visited by a cat. He excitedly told me about a new training facility for guardians down south, where they taught all kinds of advanced-level moves and tricks. But, he warned there had been some bandit attacks recently. He said that if I came and helped them fend off these ruffians, that I would be given this training right away by the resident swordmaster without being put on the waiting list, and it would be free of charge. He even mentioned medals, armor, and new weapons to go with a fancy title. What a fool I was.

I explained the offer to the king and queen, packed my things, and headed out a few days later. I'd been told to meet with the cat at a camp outside town, but I arrived to find it empty. Moments later, a hood was thrown over my head and I remembered no more. I awoke somewhere in this tower, and the witch was standing over me, laughing.

She told me I'd been cursed, that I would turn into an unstoppable monster that craved endless amounts of blood. A spell she developed herself. But, it would only happen under one condition: if I laid eyes upon the king or queen ever again."

Fiddle felt his stomach drop. Then his chest ached for the poor soul beside him as he watched him turn away and wipe his eyes.

"Maybe she was lying to you," he said. "How do you know that would really happen? Did she just let you go after that?"

"Well, she clarified by saying the triggers were actually the king, the queen, *and*... the cat I'd been lured there by. She spoke that to me even as I looked into his eyes. My vision went red, my muscles swelled, and I went after him. Seconds later, he was shredded to pieces. The witch blew dust in my face, returning me to normal, then she told me it was the last time I could change back. That's all the antidote she made, and next time the transformation would be permanent. I just had to make sure never to return to Mythland or come anywhere near the royal couple again. I attacked her, but she easily overpowered me with her dark magic. I was knocked out once more and dropped off in the wilderness.

Since then, I found the tower, but dared not come inside. I've simply done what I could for the king and queen by slaying whatever creatures I could find that were sent their way from here. I guess she thought I wouldn't be able to help myself, or I wouldn't believe her and I'd eventually go back and kill them.

Or maybe this was only a long and cruel method of torture for all of us—for doing whatever it was that angered her. I probably could've killed her in her sleep back there, you know. But even then, I was afraid she would wake up and do something horrible before my blade could land. I just want to help you find your brother and get out of here."

Fiddle was silent for a moment, then spoke, "You don't know what it means to me that you decided to join me in this forsaken place after enduring all that. Thank you, truly."

"I'm still a guardian. That's what I live for. Even if it's terrifying sometimes."

"Who's there?" came another raspy voice from high above them.

"Jak?" Fiddle called out.

"Fiddle?! Is it really you?"

"It is. I'm here with help. We're gonna get you out of here, brother."

"Pleased to meet you," said Pierre. "Though I wish it were under less grim circumstances."

"Hello to you, sir," replied Jak in an unenthusiastic tone. "There's a lever or wheel or something down there by a pillar. It lowers this cage I'm in."

Despite the darkness, Pierre located it and cranked it around with Fiddle's help.

Soon, the cage came to rest on the cold and wet stone floor. The key actually worked this lock, but the door was jammed shut. Pierre and Fiddle found a broken piece from another cage nearby and used it to pry the door open. Jak was finally free.

"Is there a different way out of here?" asked Fiddle.

"Another cat escaped his cage with my help a while back," replied Jak. "I don't know if it was hours, days, or weeks ago. But I have no idea how he got out of the tower, if he did at all."

"He did," said Pierre. "He's the reason we found you."

The three quietly discussed all that had taken place while searching around the pitch-black corners of the room for some kind of exit hole. None were found.

"I guess we have to fight our way out," said Fiddle. "By the way, I kept this warm for you."

He handed Jak his sword.

They made their way toward the entrance now—back to where the witch was hopefully still asleep, and further beyond, where a horde of her minions awaited. That's if they hadn't broken the door down by now.

When they got close enough to the soft glow of the doorway to the witch's chamber, they saw the door was sitting open. All the animals that tried attacking Pierre and Fiddle earlier were filing through, along with some extras. It was also noticed that the heavy iron door on the right was wide open, and something was coming out of it.

It was the witch herself.

She held a huge key in her hand and had a crazed and disturbing grin on her face. The key was put away somewhere within her tattered cloak and traded for a small horn. She snapped her fingers and a light near the ceiling suddenly lit the entire room.

"Finally, the day of my vengeance has come," she growled as she raised the small horn to her lips.

She blew a long, shrill, heart-freezing, eerie-sounding blast on the horn, and an immediate rumbling shook the very floor on which the cats stood.

Chapter Twelve:
A Monstrous Surprise

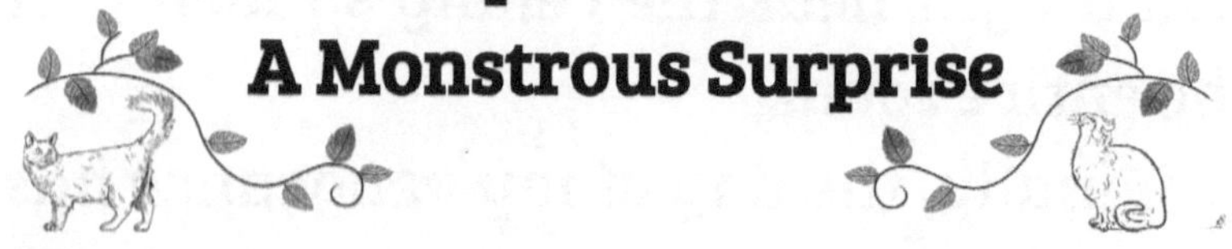

The three cats were frozen with worried anticipation. Something very large and aggressive was nearing the open doorway ahead.

They could hear the scratching, clawing, and heavy panting grow ever closer with each passing moment, and the witch's sinister smile grew with it. The crumbling ceiling rained pebbles, dust, and other debris all around, and when it seemed the thunderous rumbling could not possibly get any louder... it stopped.

The cats readied their weapons, staring at the black opening until... a huge paw with ferociously long claws stained red... reached out from the void.

It grasped the stone door frame so hard that it cracked, and soon, the other side got the same treatment from a second paw.

The tip of a long snout was slowly revealed as it silently eased out into the open room. Its massive jaws were open and dripping a yellow drool between crowded and overlapping teeth as long as daggers. Extra-long, pointed ears stood up and alert, shifting this way and that as the creature gained a sense of what lay before it.

Moments later, it had pulled itself completely out from the doorway, then stood tall on its hind legs. There was no doubt in any of the cats' minds: this was a wolf. Or at least it had been. This one seemed to have been transformed into something far more dangerous and horrifying. Parts of its dark gray, matted fur were slick with patches of blood, and its eyes gave off a faint green glow. Boney spines of varying size protruded out from all over its body—thin ones covering its back, and thicker, more jagged ones coming out from its joints and ribs. It didn't look like anything that could be alive.

Calmly, it looked to the cats on its left with a soulless, yet fully restrained rage. Then, the beastly head swung around to the witch, who stood only a few of its paces away. She was near the exit, and surrounded by her other minions.

The wolf lowered its head, as if ready to fulfill any command the old hag gave.

The witch casually strolled in a semi-circle, keeping her distance, until she came to a stop at the wall opposite of the wolf, still facing the monster.

"I have something I'd like you to do, Darkfang," she said.

Fiddle and Jak now realized who they

were looking at. It was Bayo, the wolf they'd met years ago on the way to Mythland. He'd called himself Darkfang, and Denner, his leader, had supposedly done away with him well before the attack on the castle.

"What did you do to him?" Jak called out.

The witch turned to him and replied, "He came to me just after he'd been beaten and cast out of his pack. Then he tried to force me to help him take revenge on the ones who betrayed him... which would be you and your brother. Since I don't take orders from anyone, much less a sad, foul-smelling, little reject of a dog, I locked him away. Now, he'll be able to serve a real purpose. Project Raging Venom is finally a success after all these years, and Darkfang has become my instrument of destruction. With his highly increased strength, size, and the new 'abilities' I've cursed him with, he will be used to take back what has always been rightfully mine."

"And that is?" asked Fiddle.

"Wouldn't you like to know?" she answered with narrowed eyes and another ghastly grin. "To the Mythic Castle, Darkfang! Kill The royal family! NOW! Let *NOTHING* stand in your way!!"

Darkfang turned toward the exit and broke into a run on all fours. The witch's various other minions scrambled to get away, but nearly all were trampled, crushed, skewered, slashed, and ripped to pieces before they could so much as take a step.

Then, the wolf squeezed through the door to the witch's study and smashed apart crates, bed, and shelves before bounding up the stairs.

The witch was laughing as she watched the display.

"Probably should've had some of them move first, but that was quite the entertaining sight," she said. "Besides, I can always get new helpers. How about you three?"

"We would rather die!" shouted Pierre.

"Oh, you very well might, Pierre. Then perhaps you'll be free of your own curse, at last." She gave another chuckle.

"We've got to get to the castle!" cried Fiddle.

Pierre leaned in close to him, pulling Jak in as well. "Let's surround her. Begin an attack from all sides. I'll give a signal and try to distract her with a heavy blow, and you two get out quick. I'll hold her here as long as I can. Just be careful. She can do a multitude of ranged spells, and who knows what else."

Fiddle and Jak nodded.

"We really appreciate it," said Jak.

"We can't thank you enough for all

your help," said Fiddle. "Now, let's do this."

All three of the cats yowled and hollered as they ran at the witch, with Jak on the right, Fiddle to the left, and Pierre in the center.

The witch bore no sign of surprise on her face while she put away her horn, replacing it with two other items. In her right hand was a jagged knife, and in the other, there looked to be a small and simple stick.

"Come," she said, just above a whisper, "and feel death's chilling caress."

A cloud of red and blue smoke rose from around her feet, enveloping her and obscuring the cats' view.

Fiddle saw a flash of light and jumped high as a ball of fire struck the floor beneath him. He landed in a roll, but kept running, trying to get around behind her.

Jak slid right into the magic mists,

slashing and thrusting with his sword. It hit nothing, but as soon as he stopped and began backing up, the witch exploded out of the smoke, her knife plunging down at him. He tried to parry the strike, but the witch's entire form, knife and all, dissipated into the rest of the colorful swirling clouds.

Pierre saw the exchange and came to a halt, unsure how to proceed with the fight. They wouldn't get far if the witch could not be harmed.

Fiddle could see the back of her clothing protruding from the smoke, and went for it. He ran, jumped, and brought his blade down hard.

The witch spun and deflected the strike with her knife, then hit Fiddle with a blast of electricity. He let out a wail and dropped to the floor. His vision went blurry and his chest was burning. All he could do was lie there, gasping and clutching at his chest as the dark dungeon rocked and whirled around him.

"Little!" cried Jak, becoming more furious by the moment.

He dashed back into the smoke, swinging back and forth once more, but this time, Pierre joined him.

Images of the witch's face and arms repeatedly appeared to each of them, only to vanish when their swords came into contact with her.

Then, another blast of fire flew out, singeing Pierre's left side as he threw himself out of the way.

"This isn't working!" yelled Pierre to Jak. "Just go. Get your brother out of here!"

Jak looked at Pierre one last time, then ran through the center of the smoke, slashing all around as he went. Nothing was hit, but he made it out the other side where Fiddle stay lay on the floor. So, he grabbed his brother and started dragging him towards the dungeon's exit.

Pierre saw a dark silhouette then, a raised arm holding that small stick, and a light was growing brighter at its end. He ran forward and threw his sword, one side of the double-blade finding its mark.

The witch shrieked in agony, and her next fireball curved wildly, hitting the right-side wall near the ceiling. Finally, the smoke slowly disappeared, and the witch was left standing in the open.

She spun to meet Pierre's gaze. "You *WILL* regret that!" she growled, as she tried to pull the blade from the back of her left leg.

Pierre noticed Jak pull Fiddle through the doorway and smirked, then he ran at the witch again, sliding and yanking his weapon free.

The witch screamed again and fired off multiple blasts of varying type—waves of flame, electric bolts, shards of ice, green ooze, and some sort of swirling black wind.

Pierre just barely managed to jump over, roll under, sidestep, and dodge each one before closing in for a strike. He brought up one of his blades, which was met by the witch's knife. They held that position for a moment, each pushing hard, but the witch also had her small magical stick pointed at him. The tip of it lit up, and he had no way of evading whatever was about to come at him.

'POW!'

Something glass shattered on the witch's back, creating a puff of sparkling golden smoke and sending her reeling. Pierre saw Jak's tail swish back out of the dungeon's exit. The witch's back sizzled and burned with popping and crackling noises. She twisted and swatted at it as best she could, then dropped to the floor and rolled.

Eventually, she was forced to cast off her thick outer cloak. But, as she was struggling to get her second arm through the sleeve, Pierre took his chance and came at her quickly. She barely stopped the blow since the knife was still in her free hand, but this time, Pierre rotated his weapon around and struck the stick in her other hand with the opposing blade. The stick had been caught in her sleeve, and was the reason she could not get her cloak off.

The small piece of wood was split in two, and the result was a very surprising and powerful explosion.

'BOOOOM!!'

Pierre was thrown back, flipping over several times before crashing to the wet stone floor.

He had no idea if he'd lost consciousness, or how much time had passed, but when he was able to sit up, Pierre found the witch was slowly but surely doing the same. Her whole left side was blackened and heavily wounded, and her left arm was missing up to between the elbow and shoulder. Her cloak still smoldered on the floor, and now her thin and frail-looking frame was revealed in tattered and scorched underskirts.

After getting to her feet, she looked down upon her wrecked body, and her eyes filled with hatred. She threw her knife at Pierre and missed by a considerable amount, then stumbled toward her fallen minions to look for another weapon.

A fiendish-looking, serrated sword was lifted from the floor, and she turned to face Pierre once more, looking more out of her mind than ever. She let out a terrible scream, raised the blade high, and limped toward Pierre as quickly as her injuries would allow.

"You'll not leave this tower, cat!" she hissed.

Pierre fully stood, cracked his neck a few times, readied his sword, and took a deep breath. "We'll see."

***

Jak and Fiddle had run non-stop through the night and well into the morning. The sun was high, and the brothers were beyond exhausted, but they could not stop. Darkfang was under enchantments they did not understand, and he seemed never to tire. His path of ruin was plain to see, and there was no sign of him taking any sort of break. For all they knew, he was far exceeding their pace, or had even reached the castle by now.

"I don't think I can keep going," wheezed Jak. "I feel like I'm gonna collapse."

"I know," said Fiddle. "I'm hurting pretty badly myself. Even if I didn't get a hole blown through me like I thought. But we've gotta keep moving. Every moment that we aren't is another moment that monster could be trying to kill our family."

Just then, a deer stepped out in front of the cats from between a row of bushes, causing them to slide to a halt. Fiddle recognized her as the same one he'd talked to before.

"Whoa, sorry there," she said. "Hey, I remember you. Did you find your brother?" She nodded toward Jak.

"Yes, this is him," replied Fiddle. "But now we're trying to get home in a hurry.

Our family is in serious danger. We've been running for hours and are completely worn out."

"I can take you there," said the deer. "Hop on and tell me where to go. I'm pretty quick when I need to be."

"Thank you so much," said Fiddle, and the brothers climbed onto the deer's back.

"Hold on tight," she said, then bolted away.

It wasn't long before Fiddle dozed off, and Jak had to stay awake in order to keep his brother from falling. They traded roles later that evening, and by about two hours after midnight, they arrived at the fog-shrouded gate of the Mythic Castle.

Chapter Thirteen: Fangs of Death

The gate had been torn apart, and the massive front doors of the castle itself were smashed open, with cracks and splinters jutting out from all over. One of them was just barely clinging to its last hinge, wobbling back and forth.

Most of the torches and lamps throughout the inside were already burning brightly as Fiddle and Jak passed through the entryway. They surveyed the damage but moved quickly, listening for any sign of where the monster could be. There was something faint coming from far upstairs, so they doubled their pace, believing it to be the king and queen's bedroom.

When they reached the royal

chamber, it was clear the door had been ripped off. There were sounds of sniffing and scratching coming from within.

Moving closer, Fiddle peeked inside first, laying eyes on the beast right away.

"He's just... smelling everything," he said. "I don't see bodies or blood. Hopefully, they're hidden away in one of the secret passages, or better yet, not even at home."

"What should we do?" asked Jak.

Fiddle started to answer his brother, but stopped himself when he heard a barely audible noise. It was a short and muffled cry—no doubt from the young prince. They were somewhere behind the back wall.

Most of these secret places were known about by the brothers, but they'd never had any reason to use them, nor did they know where all the entrances were.

Darkfang's ears twitched and turned in response to the noise. He sniffed at the air momentarily, then moved towards the back wall. Cabinets and tables were tossed aside to clear a path before he set his enormous claws against the hard stone that stood between him and his prey.

He tore at it first, then began repeatedly hammering it with mighty blows of his fist. Some of the stones crumbled and cracked, and though they had no idea how to stop him, the guardians of the Mythic Castle could idly watch no longer.

"HEY!!!" the two of them cried as they dashed into the room.

Fiddle leaped onto the wolf's back and held tight, stabbing into his thick hide over and over.

Jak tried to jump on as well, but missed as the wolf spun around. Instead, he rolled between the front legs and sliced them from the back. It seemed a damaging strike, but little blood was drawn, and the wolf was unfazed.

The beast set his sights on Jak, then brought his multitude of teeth down upon him. Just before snapping down, however, the wolf's head was turned aside by a side impact. It was a chair. Then, another thing hit him; this time, a vase.

The king stood in front of an open panel in the wall with the queen beside him. Each of them held pieces of furniture, ready to be thrown.

"Get away from them!!" shouted the queen.

"Right!" added the king. "Or I shall have your skin as my bathroom rug!"

Jak tried sliding out from under the wolf, but was swatted across the room. He'd only just saved himself from the claws by putting his sword in the way first.

Fiddle was soon shaken from his position on Darkfang's back, having punched hundreds of holes at that point. He hit the floor and rolled, quickly coming to his feet.

Believing he had done no harm to the wolf, he wondered if the monstrous creature was completely invincible. But a slight change was detected in his movements as he positioned himself to face the royal couple. His shoulders sagged and his breathing was labored.

Unfortunately, though, he was far from defeated.

The king drew a sword from his side, aiming it at Darkfang.

"You will leave our home at once!" he cried. "This is your last warning!"

The wolf sprung at him, jaws wide, ready to tear apart and destroy anything in their way.

The king sidestepped and slashed Darkfang's face, carving a deep gouge across a left eye that would never be used again. This caused his head to drop, and the king seized an opportunity to finish it then and there. He flipped the sword over, gripped it tightly, then plunged the tip of the blade down at the back of Darkfang's defenseless neck.

But the blade did not reach its mark. The beast's right paw caught the king in his side, sending him through the air, out the bedroom door, and into a stone wall headfirst, knocking him unconscious.

Jak and Fiddle were already back up and slashing away at the wolf's hind legs, but he ignored them as he looked to the queen.

She gasped as she got a good, close-up view of his fiery green eye, then she raised the broken leg of a table to defend herself.

"Get out of there, my queen!" cried Jak. "Run!"

He was kicked to the floor with a back leg; the wind forced out of him.

Fiddle jumped back several paces, then ran at the wolf. He let himself drop to his side, sliding up under him. When he came to a stop, he shoved his blade into the wolf's gut as hard as he could, then twisted, pulled it out, then stabbed again. Redness flowed, obscuring Fiddle's view, cutting off his air, and causing him to choke.

As he turned to spit the foul liquid out, the wolf struck him, knocking him spinning and sliding across the floor through the slick pools of crimson. He hit the wall near the door, slamming hard into the stone with his right arm, promptly dislocating it.

All the while, the queen was swinging

her table leg at the wolf's face, and he snapped back within inches of hers. Eventually, Darkfang bit down on the piece of lumber, breaking it into splinters and tossing the remains aside. The queen was cornered and unarmed.

She tried to make a quick run for it, but the wolf caught her in the top of her left shoulder near the neck with his powerful jaws, teeth sinking in deep.

The queen cried out in unbearable, searing, explosive pain, then screamed, "Jak! Help me!"

The sounds of her voice filled Jak with a renewed strength. Adrenaline coursed through his veins like hot bolts of lightning. As he got himself to a standing position, he saw Fiddle's blood-soaked sword slide over, coming to rest at his feet. He picked it up and glanced at his brother, who was wincing and holding his right arm.

Jak turned to Darkfang, then sprinted, jumped, and ran up the wolf's back. He used the swords to climb faster, alternating stabs into the already bloody hide and pushing himself up towards the head as the wolf dropped the queen and stood upright. She collapsed to the floor with a 'thud' and continued to holler and writhe in agony, her voice growing weak from the overwhelming torment.

Darkfang thrashed about, trying to throw Jak off, but the cat held on tight as he approached his first target. The moment the wolf paused, Jak leaped and slammed both swords down into the back of his neck. For the first time, the wretched beast gave an indication of hurt. He howled with a deep, guttural, echoing, unholy fury that rattled windows and shook stone down to the very foundations of the castle.

The wolf wildly spun and twisted

about, crashing into walls and swiping madly at his own back in vain, for his arms could not reach. He stumbled over to the center of the room, and once there, Jak spotted something that gave him an idea. But he had to be quick.

Jak ripped the swords out from the beast's neck, then ran up the back of his head, jumping straight upward when reaching the end of his snout. He passed through the center of a round chandelier with dozens of candles burning all around, then grabbed the rope which held it affixed to the ceiling.

"Little!" he called out to his brother. "The lamp! Throw the lamp!!"

Fiddle looked up to an end table beside him, and there sat a glass lamp filled with oil. It was not burning, but it didn't need to be.

With a swift slash, Jak cut the rope below the place he held it, and the chandelier dropped. He watched as it fell and slipped perfectly over Darkfang's body, just as the glass lamp shattered against his mutilated back, covering him in oil.

Immediately, the wolf was engulfed in flames and let out another quaking howl. But it wasn't enough for Jak. He let go of the severed rope and plummeted toward the flames, punching both swords into Darkfang's upturned throat. The blades tore two deep gashes from the wolf's chin to his chest, which sent him into a frenzy unlike anything before.

Within two bounds, the wolf crossed the room and smashed through a large window with Jak still holding on. The burning monster flipped end over end, falling forty feet before crashing into the garden pond, sending water spraying and smoke billowing. Then, all went still and quiet.

A few minutes later, Fiddle came limping through the hazy moonlit garden, approaching the pond as fast as he was able.

He saw the wolf's back sticking up from the surface of the water just in front of him, hesitating only a moment before proceeding to see if he could locate his brother.

"Jak!" he called out to the dark, rippling water.

"Yeah?" answered a voice to his right.

It was Jak, slid up against a small tree and soaked to the bone.

"Oh, thank goodness," said Fiddle. "I thought you were still trapped underneath him."

"Well, I had to make sure he didn't run off with *these*," Jak replied, motioning to the two swords that lay beside him on the grass.

"Right. That would've been a heck of a

shame, for sure. So, is he...?"

"Dead? Yes, I'm quite certain."

"Good job, man. You were amazing. But we've still got problems, as I'm sure you know. The queen is in bad shape. We should get back up there right away."

Jak stood, walked over to his brother, wrapped his arms around him, then body-slammed him in the side of his right shoulder. A loud 'pop' was heard, and Fiddle yelped, nearly retching in pain and disgust.

"You're welcome," said Jak. "Now, let's get moving."

The cats circled the castle, entered, and ascended the stairs once more. Back in the royal chamber, the king was not only awake, but on his feet and carrying the queen to their bed.

He lay her down gently and visibly fought back his first instincts of becoming hysterical. Gritting his teeth, he looked to his guards; his adopted sons, who now joined him beside the bed.

"The beast is dead," said Jak.

The king nodded, face unchanging, then replied, "She's getting worse by the second. I wrapped the wound and stopped the bleeding, but something else is ravaging her body, like a sickness or curse."

Fiddle's eyes went wide.

"Project Raging Venom," he mumbled.

The king turned to him with a look of bewilderment, but Jak had an idea of what it meant.

"What an idiot I've been," Fiddle continued. "I was reading through the witch's notes on this very thing, but thought it wasn't important at the time and stopped just before reading what claimed to be some sort of cure. I should have grabbed it on the way out. It was a magical venom that Darkfang was cursed with, and it's likely the only way to undo it lies within the pages of that book in the witch's tower. I need to get back there."

"Do you think you could ride a horse?" asked the king. "Our drivers are asleep in their homes, and I don't think she's going to make it much longer."

"We'll have to try," answered Fiddle. "We rode a deer earlier. How different can it be? I'm just hoping the witch didn't survive... the uh... thrashing we gave her."

"Yes, let's hope," said the king. "I'll run down and get one ready." He then turned and jogged out the door.

Fiddle and Jak watch the queen for a time; her chest shuddered with each breath, which came in awful crackling wheezes. The uncovered area around the wound on her shoulder and neck was swollen and yellow, with veins turning dark. Her eyes were fully open, bloodshot, and unresponsive, aside from occasional twitching. Her skin was drenched with sweat, hot to the touch, and deathly pale.

The brothers thought she might slip away before the king could even make it back up the steps, but moments later, he came rushing through the door again.

"All ready to go," he said, panting. "Just out front. Do hurry."

"We'll be back soon," said Jak, but a hand grasped his arm as he turned away.

"Stay... Buddy," said the queen. "Please."

Jak looked at her, then to his brother, who placed a paw on his shoulder.

"Keep her safe," said Fiddle. "I've got this."

Jak nodded, and Fiddle gave the queen a final glance before running out the door.

Chapter Fourteen:
A Grave Decision

"If anything comes after you, just run," said Fiddle. "Keep circling the tower until you see me come out."

"I can do that," said the dark brown horse. "Be careful in there, would you?"

"Of course."

Fiddle made his way up the short set of steps leading to the front entrance of the witch's tower. The door was still sitting open, just how he and Jak had left it days earlier. He heard no sounds, save for the wind in the trees and the song of a single, distant bird.

The royal stallion that bore him had made great time, arriving at their destination in just under six hours. It was not even ten in the morning yet, and

Fiddle hoped to be back at the queen's side by dinner time with a cure.

As he passed through the front door, he couldn't help but notice some pink splotches on the stone floor below. They seemed to be growing darker, turning more red as he followed them down the stairs to the dungeon. He realized they were bloody cat prints. They must have been from Pierre.

He reached the witch's study and found it to be in much the same shape as he'd seen it last. Darkfang had made a mess of the room, knocking most of its contents out of place and smashing many an object beyond recognition on his brief passage through.

Fiddle was certainly in a hurry, but he had to take a peek into the dungeon and see if there was any evidence of how the fight with the witch ended, and to make sure nothing was in there ready to sneak up on him as he completed his task.

He stepped through the ruined doorway, covering his nose and mouth from a sudden, terrible smell. The wreckage of minions' bodies were all around as expected, but in the center of the area was another, quite different body; one which Fiddle approached with caution.

There before him, in a pool of red, lay the witch. Her eyes were rolled back, her mouth hung wide open, and there was a devastating wound in her belly. Flies buzzed about her, and the odor emanating from her body was indescribable. There was no reason to believe she could still be alive, but Fiddle reluctantly took a step forward, held his breath, and poked at her with his blade. She was stiff as a log, and deader than cold stone. Pierre had put an end to her.

After a quick fit of vomiting, Fiddle

returned to the witch's study. It took him a few minutes, but he found the item he was looking for in the corner of the room under a pile of debris. Only... now it was closed. On the cover of the black book was simply written 'Projects'.

Fiddle flipped through the pages, starting from the beginning, looking for the specific page he'd seen before. Every few pages, names of unknown and likely atrocious designs appeared in bold letters at the top, always beginning with the word 'project'.

He quickly and quietly read each one aloud as he frantically searched for the right one.

"Project Black Hail. Project Ironwall. Project Stormhawk. Project Crimson Razor. Project Soundquake. Project Flaming Trumpet. Project Stopclock. Project Nightvermin. Project Hyperkey. Project Bog Slime. Project Necrocrystal.

Project Meteor Blade. Project Ashen Winter. Project Raging Venom. Project Butterca—Hey! That was it!"

He flipped back a few pages and found exactly what he'd come for, but his joy faded as he read the words. There was a way, but it wasn't a simple one.

He tore the page out, folded it up, and shoved it in a small pouch on his sword belt. Then he located the only artifact necessary to perform the curse removal: a wide and sharp knife which looked to be carved from bone. It may have even been the tooth of some tremendous beast. Either way, Fiddle had what he needed, and swiftly exited the tower.

The brown horse raised his head upon hearing Fiddle's approach, still chewing a tuft of grass.

"We ready to go?" he asked.

Fiddle gave an unenthusiastic nod, then climbed atop the horse's back.

Within moments, they were speeding back through the Palemist Wood, leaving the tower shrinking below treetops behind them.

***

The king held his infant son, fighting back his emotions as he watched his daughter have what he believed to be the final moments with her dying mother. Jak and a doctor from the town stood beside her, neither one of them able to do anything to help her.

Fiddle rushed in just then, and the doctor stepped out to give them space.

"Did you find it, Little?" asked the king with hardly any hope left in his expression.

"I did," he answered. "But the way it's done is... complicated."

"It doesn't matter," said Jak. "We'll do

whatever it takes."

Fiddle took a deep breath, then explained the procedure, showing to them the knife that was supposedly crucial to the curse's undoing.

"Someone has to take this knife... and stab her in the area she received the bite." The king and Jak began to speak at the same time, but Fiddle cut them off.

"This does *not* get rid of the curse. It only transfers it to the person holding the knife. Once it's done, it says the knife will crumble to ash, preventing any further use. So, the person who does this will simply take her place, and probably won't live to see tomorrow."

The king's face was filled with horror and sorrow.

"Let me take the kids to their room," he said. "Then we can continue this discussion."

Fiddle patted the princess on the back

as she was led away, then moved closer to the queen to get a better look at her.

He wouldn't have thought it possible before, but her appearance had worsened considerably since he'd last seen her. The bruised yellow skin and blackened veins had spread down her left arm and up the side of her face, and her breathing was nearly non-existent. Her death was imminent, and Fiddle wondered if she'd survive even if the curse was completely removed from her body.

Then he looked to his brother, whose eyes stared back, stricken with anguish, but still holding a glimmer of determination. The two of them said nothing as they awaited the return of the king.

"Alright," said the king, stepping back into the room. "Can we get someone else to do it? Someone evil, perhaps?"

"Maybe," replied Fiddle. "But who could we find? She looks like she could slip away at any moment. I don't believe that's a possibility. But I will say this. I am ready and willing to do it myself."

The king and Jak suddenly grew almost offended.

"I am her husband," said the king with a hint of command in his voice. "If anyone should take her place, it is I."

"No!" yelled Jak. "I am her personal guard. It's my actual job to keep her from harm. It needs to be me. Hand me the blade."

"Wait," said Fiddle. "This can't be the only way. We need to think."

"There's no time!" shouted the king. "Give it here! That's an order!"

"I am sworn to protect you!" cried Fiddle, pulling the knife away from him. "I cannot allow you to do this."

The king came at him anyway, but

soon found himself consumed by a blanket Jak had thrown off the bed.

Jak tripped the king as he stumbled, then rolled him over and pinned the blanket to the floor with his sword. The shouting and kicking that followed were ignored as Jak turned to find Fiddle standing on the bed with knife in hand. He ran, jumped, and body slammed his brother, knocking him over the queen to the far side of the bed.

"You can't!" yelled Jak as he pounced on Fiddle and began prying the knife from his paws.

"No, you can't!" screamed Fiddle. "I won't let you!"

Jak smiled, then punched Fiddle hard in the gut and yanked the knife away.

"You don't have to let me," he said. "But this is what I was born to do—what I'm here for—and nothing is going to keep me from it."

With one swift motion, he twisted, brought the knife overhead, and sent it plunging down into the queen's shoulder.

The swelling flesh, yellowed skin, and black veins all receded at once, flowing through the knife and changing it from white to black. It momentarily flashed green, then turned to dust in Jak's paw.

The life returned to the queen's face, and she gasped a breath of fresh air and sat upright. She looked into Jak's eyes as he stood beside her. He smiled, then collapsed across her lap, wheezing and choking.

The king was back on his feet, rushing to the bed, and Fiddle crawled over to sit beside the queen.

She took Jak in her arms and held him close, knowing what had been done.

"Why did you do this?" she asked. "I didn't want you to sacrifice yourself for me!"

Jak trembled, barely able to whisper an answer.

"You gave me a better life than I would've ever imagined possible. Saving yours was the least I could do."

Tears streamed from the queen's eyes as she felt his body shudder.

"I love you, Buddy," she said, stroking his head.

"And I you, my lady."

Jak pulled in a sharp gasp, shuddering again. Then he let out a long, soft exhale, and moved no more.

The queen's anguish could be felt throughout all of Mythland.

Chapter Fifteen: A Greeting and a Farewell

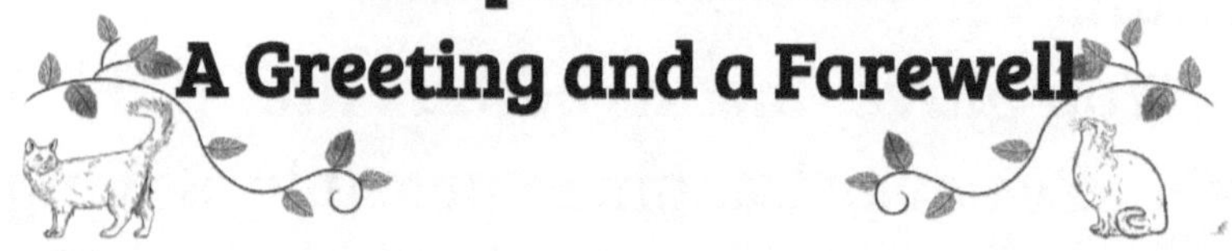

The afternoon sun shone down upon the queen's garden where the royal couple stood with their children two days after Jak's passing.

Darkfang's body had been removed, hauled away and burned. The water in the pond was then replaced and the rest of the garden tidied in preparation for the funeral.

Fiddle knelt by the recently filled grave, his outstretched paw placed against the front of the headstone. Engraved on it were the words:

SIR JAK THE CHIVALROUS
Beloved Brother
Loving Son
Brave Knight
Guardian of the Mythic Castle
May you rest in eternal peace.

Fiddle looked over the inscription, then whispered to himself.

"I would've treated you with the honor you truly deserved if I'd only known how short of a time I was going to have with you. I know I could be a real jerk sometimes... and I'm sorry. As a brother and a fellow guardian, you were the best."

He stood, then made his way over to stand with his family, the king setting a hand on his shoulder.

They stayed out in the garden until nightfall, talking of the past and telling stories about Jak. Most were even able to smile at times when recalling some of his more humorous moments. But, just as the past two nights had been, each member of the family, save for the very young prince, had trouble getting to sleep. It all seemed so unbelievable; their minds could not accept that Jak was truly gone and never coming back.

There was a short relief in slumber, if the dreams stayed far away from reality, but upon waking, the truth always came flooding back in.

Many weeks passed before the family could face the normal routine of life as usual, but there were always reminders.

The king, the queen, and Fiddle each felt responsible at times in their own way, and believed it should have been them instead of him. But nothing could be done about that now, no matter how much they wished for it.

Fiddle even struggled for a time to feel as if he still belonged there, as if he didn't deserve to live in the comfort of the castle any longer while his brother was buried outside under the dirt.

He even went away for a while on several occasions, feeling somewhat guilty about leaving the castle unguarded, but desperately needing some time to himself. Despite wanting to be alone, he found himself searching for Pierre on his travels, but much to his dismay, not a trace of him could be found.

Over a year later, he continued taking his once-a-month-or-so weekend-long journeys, as he came to call them.

On one particular trip, he happened to be walking near the eastern outskirts of the Palemist Wood, not even considering going inside it. He'd break off soon and head further east, maybe visit Ronaldsburg and see a mind-numbing stage play.

However, as he began moving further away from the treeline, his ears caught the sound of a terrible racket coming from within the forest; a screeching and shrieking mixed with what seemed to be frightened cries. He turned and jogged back, then stopped to listen again.

"Help! Help me, please! Anyone!" came a voice amidst whatever was causing those shrieking sounds.

Fiddle got low and rushed into the woods, following the noises to a great tree. A huge, black bird was furiously digging at a hollowed out spot at the base of the tree, the place from which the cries for help came. But this was no ordinary bird. Not only was it one of the mutated beasts belonging to the witch, it also was missing part of its right leg. This was the very creature that had kidnapped his brother and taken him to the witch's tower.

Anger burned inside Fiddle, but he didn't want to risk getting picked up and flown away like he might if he just ran in waving his sword. So instead, he silently crept wide around the bird, sticking to shadows and bushes until he came to the back side of the tree it continued tearing into.

Fiddle climbed the tree, found a good spot around twenty feet up, then dropped a large stick to the ground on the bird's left side. When the feathered beast stretched out its neck to inspect the suspicious branch, Fiddle jumped from his perch.

"Eat crap, you deformed turkey!!" screamed Fiddle as his blade passed clean through the animal's neck.

Fiddle hit the ground with a roll at the same time the bird's head landed. He immediately jumped to his feet and observed the decapitated body wobbling around on its one foot. A well-placed kick from Fiddle sent it tumbling over into the grass, where it flopped about for a while.

"You can come out," said Fiddle. "It's safe now."

A thin black cat emerged from the crack in the tree, shaking uncontrollably and looking to be on the verge of starvation.

"Th-thank you, sir," he said. "How can I repay you?"

"Repay me? I *wanted* to kill that darned thing. And aside from whatever that is on your collar that I don't want or need, it doesn't look like you're in a position to be paying for anything."

"Right."

The two cats stared at each other for an uncomfortable amount of time before Fiddle broke the silence.

"Welp... bye then."

He turned away, but the black cat shouted out in a panic.

"W-wait! Can I walk with you for a bit? I've been trying to survive out here for a long time, and I'd like some decent company. Or, if you could just point me in the direction of a town, I'd—"

"Yeah, sure," interrupted Fiddle while pulling out some meat sticks. "I was heading towards a town anyway. Take some of these and... well... walk alongside me, I guess. Just try not to slow down too much or we won't make it before the rest of my food runs out."

"Thank you so much."

"Uh-huh. Keep aware that I'll be watching you. Don't try anything funny or you'll regret ever meeting me. Got it?"

"Absolutely, sir. You haven't a thing to worry about! My name's Popeil, by the way. Some just call me Pope."

"Cool.... I'm called Fiddle. I'm a guardian knight from Mythland."

"Fiddle?! You're the brother of that cat I was locked in the dungeon with!"

"Oh, it's you, huh? I guess I should be thanking *you* then. Your message was passed to me by a gray cat I met. It was the only reason I was able to find my brother in time. Not that it even matters much at this point."

"Did something happen?"

"One of the witch's experiments got him. He's been gone for over a year now."

"I'm so sorry to hear that."

"Yeah, me too. But listen, don't think I trust you any more just because your info helped me out back then. You *are* one of those experiments as far as I'm concerned. Who knows what she did to you...."

"I can assure you, I am not a danger. It's fine if you're suspicious, but I really need to get out of here."

Fiddle looked long and hard at him. "Alright. Let's go then."

The cats walked through the night and arrived in Ronaldsburg the following morning. There, they saw a terribly boring play, ate at a somewhat fancy restaurant, and loaded themselves down with plenty of supplies. All on Fiddle's coin, of course.

As evening came, Fiddle said his goodbyes to Popeil, not regretting the encounter with him, but glad to be back on his own once more. Two days later, and Fiddle had returned to the Mythic Castle. His whole family was gathered out by the gate to greet him.

"Always good to see you back home safe, Little," said the king, catching him in a hug.

"I got into a bit of a scuffle, but it was nothing I couldn't handle," he replied while embracing the queen, the prince, and princess all at the same time.

He wondered if he should tell them of the black cat, Popeil. But his thoughts were cut short when the king shouted out.

"Who's your friend?!"

Fiddle turned to see Pope peeking around a small tree on the opposite side of the road. He rolled his eyes in annoyance.

"Oh, just some guy I met out in the wild. I also may have saved his life. He knew Jak and—"

"Are you kidding me?" cried the king. "That's great! Hey, fellow, come along over here and quit sneaking around. Let's get the two of you inside and put some real food in your bellies. What do you say?"

"That sounds wonderful," said Pope, taking the queen by the hand and introducing himself.

Fiddle rubbed at his forehead, then fell in line as the family moved up the path to the front door. He leaned close to Pope as they walked and whispered in his ear.

"I've still got my eye on you, weirdo. After dinner, I'm gonna need you to excuse yourself and get the heck right out of here."

"We've got plenty of extra rooms if you need a place to stay," said the queen.

Fiddle thought he was going to get sick. He did not want this cat here, decent or otherwise. He began to protest, but kept his mouth shut, figuring he'd just drop it for now. Like he'd said, though, he was going to be watching this fellow closely. One wrong move and he'd be out on his backside.

"So, what's for dinner?" Fiddle asked as the door shut behind them.

In Loving Memory of Jak aka "Buddy Man"
April 2008 – October 2013